Praise for Juan José Saer

"[*La Grande*] is a daring, idiosyncratic work that examines the idea of an individual person navigating the whirl of random events that helps shape everyone's lives."–*Kirkus Review* (starred)

"The most striking element of Saer's writing is his prose, at once dynamic and poetic. . . . It is brilliant."–*Harvard Review*

"Brilliant. . . . With meticulous prose, rendered by Dolph's translation into propulsive English, Saer's *The Sixty-Five Years of Washington* captures the wildness of human experience in all its variety."
–*New York Times*

"What Saer presents marvelously is the experience of reality, and the characters' attempts to write their own narratives within its excess."
–*Bookforum*

"A cerebral explorer of the problems of narrative in the wake of Joyce and Woolf, of Borges, of Rulfo and Arlt, Saer is also a stunning poet of place."–*The Nation*

"To say that Juan José Saer is the best Argentinian writer of today is to undervalue his work. It would be better to say that Saer is one of the best writers of today in any language."–Ricardo Piglia

Also by Juan José Saer

The Clouds
The Event
The Investigation
La Grande
Nobody Nothing Never
Scars
The Sixty-Five Years of Washington
The Witness

Juan
José
Saer

The
One
Before

*Translated from the Spanish
by Roanne L. Kantor*

OPEN LETTER
LITERARY TRANSLATIONS FROM THE UNIVERSITY OF ROCHESTER

Library of Congress Cataloging-in-Publication Data:

Saer, Juan José, 1937-2005 author.
    [Short stories. Selections]
    The one before / by Juan Jose Saer ; Translated from the Spanish by
Roanne L. Kantor. — First edition.
        pages cm
    "Originally published in Spanish as La mayor, 1976."
    ISBN 978-1-934824-78-8 (pbk. : alk. paper) — ISBN 1-934824-78-X (pbk. : alk. paper)
    I. Kantor, Roanne L. translator. II. Saer, Juan José, 1937-2005 One before.
III. Saer, Juan José, 1937-2005 One before English. IV. Title.
    PQ7797.S22435M313 2015
    863'.64—dc23
                                        2014043782

Printed on acid-free paper in the United States of America.

Text set in Bodoni, a serif typeface first designed by Giambattista
Bodoni (1740–1813) in 1798.

Design by N. J. Furl

Open Letter is the University of Rochester's nonprofit, literary translation press:
Lattimore Hall 411, Box 270082, Rochester, NY 14627

www.openletterbooks.org

For Adolfo Prieto

A pilgrim's footsteps always wander
–Luis de Góngora, *Los soledades*

Contents

Translator's Note   ix

·

Arguments   3

A Layman's Thoughts on Painting   5

Regarding a Literary Argument   6

The Biography of Higinio Gómez   8

The Interpreter   10

Scent Memory   13

A Historian's Insomnia   15

The Septuagenarian Poet   17

The Lookalike   19

Argument over the Term Zone   22

Anonymous Biography   25

Hands and Planets   27

The Mourner   30

Regarding Autumn Siestas   32

Friends   34

Beaches   37

Gandia's Bar   39

White Hot   41

A Change of Residence   44

Veiled   46

The Mirror   48

My Name is Pigeon Garay   50

Memories   51

The Traveler   54

Abroad   60

The Scattering   62

The Body   63

On Dry Shore   64

Letter to the Seer   70

Half-Erased   73

The One Before   117

•

Translator's Acknowledgments   149

Translator's Note

Soon after completing the translation you are about to read, I was invited to speak at a conference on Saer in Buenos Aires. The panel was titled, rather provocatively, "Is It Possible to Translate Juan José Saer?"

I leave this question for the reader to judge. What I can say with certainty is that Saer's writing generally, and *The One Before* in particular, is deeply concerned with the theme of translation and its limits. This includes, of course, a few examples of straightforward linguistic translation, as in the case of Filipillo, the young indigenous man conscripted as a translator for the Spanish conquistadors in "The Interpreter." More often, however, Saer's concern with translation is manifest in larger questions about the possibility of representing human experience in any language. Stories like "On Dry Shore," "The Lookalike," and "Friends" speak to his hope that writing would be adequate to the task of preserving a particular moment or a particular perspective on the world. Others suggest profound doubt about the ability of language to capture these moments, and the sneaking suspicion that the coherence imposed on human memory by the narrative form is, at bottom, a mirage.

These ideas reach their pinnacle in the titular story, "The One Before." An unidentified narrator, probably the recurring character Carlos Tomatis, becomes increasingly disoriented as he recalls the same set of events over and over again, gradually losing his faith in the relationship between successive moments in time. Here Saer takes up the challenge he lays out in another story, "Memories." The task is to create a narrative that is authentic to memory itself—a "circular narrative" in which the "position of the narrator would be like that of a boy who, riding a horse on a merry-go-round, tries at each pass to snatch a steel loop from the ring." And yet *The One Before* is also a text that relies on the coherence of memory, citing and even playfully translating others, most notably Marcel Proust and Maurice Merleau-Ponty.

We might also understand this collection to refer to translation at its etymological origins—to move from one place to another. The stories "Argument Over the Term 'Zone'," "Abroad," "A Change of Residence," and others reflect on the dislocation Saer experienced when he moved permanently from Santa Fe to Paris in 1968. "Half-Erased" explores this theme through the perspective of another recurring character in Saer's oeuvre, Pigeon Garay. In the story, Pigeon spends the last days in the city of his birth searching fruit-lessly for his twin brother, Cat, while a catastrophic flood pro-gressively obliterates the familiar landscape around them. Decades later, Pigeon will return to Santa Fe in the novel *The Investigation*, only to find that the erasures of his initial "translation" can never be undone.

In his famous and oft-cited essay on translation, "The Task of the Translator," Walter Benjamin writes, "A real translation is trans-parent; it does not cover the original, does not block its light, but allows the pure language, as though reinforced by its own medium, to shine upon the original all the more fully." Borrowing Saer's own words from "Letter to the Seer," I close the introduction to these stories with the hope that I have let his light shine in them, if, indeed, one of the modes of his writing is to shine.

The
One
Before

Arguments

A Layman's Thoughts on Painting

I think more about frames than paintings. My preference: altar-pieces and images of the Way of the Cross. Between each station on the Way of the Cross is the empty wall. It goes unrecognized as the true frame holding in the pathetic magic of feeling without allowing it to spill from its borders toward the ocean of oil that is indeterminacy. The frame shows that Christ was crucified; it preserves his sacrifice for us and saves us from the confusion of his hesitations, his stubbornness, and his fear. We owe the frame perspective, perfect profiles, and the most surprising accomplishment of painting: concrete abstraction.

The docent of the municipal museum thinks I'm crazy because he's seen me looking at the empty wall. It looks white in the sense of white-hot; the red, symbol of heat and passion, becomes invisible through abundance and excess. So much of the same feeling neutralizes itself and blinds the rest and then we feel unworthy to keep looking. How can I explain such a thing to my friends who are painters? Each picture looks to me like a white wall that has been diminished, attenuated. Perhaps the word "cut" would serve, as when we say to cut wine with water. Thus, the art of painting is for me the art of reduction. Let us honor the frame, because from uniformity it creates the variety of the passion. Rainbows reign in the sky for a moment and then fade, in the afternoon, into the arms of a night darker and more indistinguishable than fire.

Regarding a Literary Argument

We began nice and early in the morning. When, seven hours later, we were still arguing after having eaten lunch, something in the room was different, and I'm not talking about the light that had changed over time, or about the cigarette smoke, or about the notes or abstract doodles which now sullied papers that once were white. Arguments at the height of summer! I know what I'm talking about, but the more I try, the less able I am to say it. It's a state of the world so uncertain and banal that no one has ever invented a term to adequately describe it. Perhaps nothing really is happening and I, purely out of vertigo, have set about trying to pin down some unnamable thing in the very center of nothingness. But let's just say that something happened: not the smoke, nor the papers, nor the light, nor the tables, nor the people, nor the themes up for discussion were the same as they had been at nine in the morning. Baroque variants: there was never any morning, or rather, this moment stands alone, the word "was" is only real when it is said (you might say it's nothing more than a sound), and now there is nothing more than the great wide space where everything is clear, as I see it now, freshly sprouted and swarming, what we call the present.

Well directed, a single example can serve to suggest diversity, even infinity. We, members of a cultural commission, discussed the possibility of updating and disseminating, for the public benefit of the city, a classic work—Cervantes, let's say. We split up the basic ideas of *Don Quijote*, a product of fundamental facts. First, to order it historically, is the great envelope into which we were born and which we call the world, one of whose parts is the general opinion that *Don Quijote* is a masterpiece. (Another of its parts is *Don Quijote*, naturally.) The second fact is our reading of *Don Quijote*. I like to compare this reading to the times I spent hours playing with a mirror, making the sunlight bounce off of its smooth surface, filling up the room with mobile stains of light and dazzling glimmers. Seven hours after we began, the two suppositions have gotten so far away from our immediate experience that, without suggesting that they have been erased, I would venture to say that their relation to our debate is the same as the foundation of a house to its architectural style and the arrangement of its rooms; it sustains them, but no one sees it, and no one has ever seen it besides the engineers who constructed it. At the mouth of the tunnel of warm weather that has passed since this morning, what the world knows about Cervantes and *Don Quijote* is now filled in, densely, opaquely, no less arid than the arid walls our voices echoed against, nor less compact than the words that fall continually from our brains to our mouths and raise continually from the air to our minds. And once again I begin to feel that something is changing, without knowing what, without knowing how to express it, or knowing if it is even really changing, without knowing if I am able or if it would be worthwhile to say so, if it is true that it has really changed. With just one step one could pass from this state of strangeness into horror. From here the possibility of writing a new classic is almost nil: that's why I said an argument on the edge of summer.

The Biography of Higinio Gomez

Higinio Gomez was born in a house within view of the Parana River, in 1915. It was a weekend cottage, because at that time wealthy people sought out the river. He was an only child. His mother died in childbirth and, when Higinio was ten, his father, who wanted to teach him to ride a horse, to "make a man out of him," drunkenly mounted one and got himself killed. Higinio's tutor sold the weekend house and packed Higinio off to an English school in Buenos Aires. Every three months he got a visit from his aunts. When he turned eighteen he left school and went to Europe. He wandered around, had a fling with an English girl, and met Andre Breton and the men he hung around with. Once in a while he attended poetry classes given by Paul Valery at the Collège de France. One night in April he participated in a literary discussion that turned into a fistfight and produced another, more serious schism in the Surrealist movement, and then, tired, he took a steamer back to Buenos Aires, just before World War II. He told some friends that being abroad made him dizzy, like wine, and by the time he found his tutor, who by then was blind, he realized he didn't have a cent left. Botana's wife got him a job at *Critica*, which was already on the decline. He argued with the other journalists over the impossibility of loving anyone after twenty-five—he thought about the English girl as he spoke, without his interlocutors ever realizing—but really he knew that, for his part, there was little or nothing left to do. "My penis," he used to say to those closest to him, "is like a deflated balloon." And other times, "No insurance company would give me a policy that could secure my genitals." He wrote narrative poems, extremely long ones. Tomatis, who later compiled and wrote an introduction to a compilation of Higinio's poems—"The Beach" and "Regions"—said there were a mountain of aphorisms among his papers, all written, funnily enough, in pencil. Tomatis had a hard time deciphering them because they were already half erased. One of them said that it would be easier to fall off of a horse and die than to find someone worth loving, even for someone who lived in a world without horses. Another aphorism, according to Tomatis, said that women die in childbirth from remorse, and a third that poetry is not a majestic and fertile river, but a rock standing firm in the current, polished by the water.

Carlos Tomatis had the privilege of getting to know his manuscripts because one afternoon in February an old actress who had been Higinio's friend in Buenos Aires turned up at the office of the newspaper *La Region* and practically put a gun to his head to get him take on the project. She was accompanied by an old man dressed in a brick-colored polo shirt, jeans, and sandals. Thanks to the actress, since the old man didn't deign to open his mouth, Tomatis devoted himself to the project and saw to the publication of the compilation. Higinio had returned to the city around 1960 and was somewhat involved in the literary scene, but two years later he rented a hotel room and poisoned himself. He left behind the aphorisms and a mountain of narrative poems in which he spoke of a yellow river and mocked the transparency of the ocean.

The Interpreter

Now I am walking along the shore of the ocean, upon sand that is smoother and more yellow than fire. When I stop and look behind me, I see the border of my crisscrossing footprints intricately traversing the beach and coming to rest just beneath my toes. The white, intermittent border of foam separates the yellow expanse of the beach from the sky-blue of the water. If I look at the horizon, I feel that I will begin to see, again, the butchering boats advancing from the ocean toward the coast, black dots at first, then strained filigrees, and finally pot-bellied casks supporting the sails, and a forest of masts and cables slipping taught out front, gradually revealing a throng of active men. When I saw them, I closed my eyes against the shine of their stony breastplates, and the sound of metal and of harsh voices deafened me for a moment. I was ashamed of our rough and humble cities and I understood that they counted for nothing, nor did Ataliba's gold and emeralds (which they pulverized with hammers searching for the meat, as one does with a nut), nor the huge paved corridors walled with silver, nor our immense stone calendars, nor the imperial guard that reappears, time and again, on our façades, in the garments of the court and on our earthenware. I saw an open stream of abundance and glory flow forth from the sea. With a cross, the butchers touched the forehead of the child I used to be, gave me a new name, Filipillo, and then, slowly, they taught me their language. I made it out, gradually, and the words advanced toward me, Filipillo, from the horizon where they filled in, layered upon each other to become, again, like the boats, black dots, black iron filigrees, and finally a forest of crosses, symbols, masts, and cables pouring out from a boiling mound like terrified ants from an anthill. Then I was no longer the naked child whose eyes sparkled with the metal of armor and whose ears echoed, for the first time, with the roar of the sails, and I began to be Filipillo, the man endowed with a double tongue, like a snake's. From my mouth came the blessing, the poison, the ancient word my mother used to call me in the afternoon, from among the bonfires and the smoke and the smell of food wafting along the streets of the brick-colored city, and those sounds that echo in me like in a bottomless, empty well. My life is always swinging between the words my voice rips from my blood, and the learned words my mouth devours greedily at another's table, tracing a parabola that sometimes erases the line of demarcation. I feel as if I am passing through a region of alternately nocturnal and diurnal zones, like a rooster crowing at an unearthly hour, like the jester who improvises for Ataliba, before the laughter of the court, a song not of words, but simply of sound.

When the butchers judged Ataliba, I was the interpreter. Words passed through me like the words of God pass through a priest before reaching the populace. I was the white line, unstable, agitated, that separated two formidable armies, like the border of foam separating the yellow sand from the ocean; and my body was the feverish loom where destiny was woven from a throng with the double needle of my tongue. Words flew like arrows and pierced me, reverberating. Had I understood the same thing they told me? Had I given the same thing I received? When my eyes, during the judgment, fell upon the blue breasts of Ataliba's wife, breasts that might permit, perhaps, in the absence of Ataliba's hand, a visit from my greedy fingers, had this disturbance disfigured the meaning of the words that resounded in the immobile enclosure? I'm sure of one thing: that my tongue was like a double tray upon whose elastic plates conspiracy and lies sat in comfort. I felt the roar of the two armies, like two oceans joining, an ocean of blood and a foreign ocean of black water, and now, in the afternoon, I walk along the beach, an old man bent under the vault of enemy voices that extend interminably over my ruins, consumed by the jungle. Like one sucked into a stream of water, only to be gargled and spit back out again, I didn't die with those who died when I handed down the sentence, but nor do I live the fierce life of the butchers whose voices are carried to me on the wind at night, when I go to sleep in the jungle.

When the butchers began to build their city, they made a thick wall of adobe and painted it white. But one part of it crumbled and they abandoned it. That white wall remained in the middle of a bare field, and at noon the light shines on its white surface pockmarked by the open air. Sometimes I sit on the ground and look at it, for hours. I think that the butcher's language, for me, is like this wall, compact, useless, meaningless, and I am blinded when the light reflects against its corrupt and arid face. A wall to scratch until my fingers bleed, or to crash against, but with no house behind where I could go in and enjoy the shade. I am nothing but an old Indian wandering the jungle in silence, among the ruins, and I can no longer hear, in the afternoon, my mother's voice calling me home from among the bonfires and the smoke and the smell of food wafting along the streets of a brick-colored city that extended to the sky.

Scent Memory

In the interior, these days, you can't be an empiricist, even if you have reached the age of sixty-six and teach philosophy classes at the University. I say that you can't be an empiricist for this reason especially, most especially if you have three children (the eldest also a professor of philosophy, but in Canada), eight grandchildren, and a wife who follows you around the whole blessed day with wool socks, because she knows that at this point catching cold can be deadly. And nevertheless, it is old age, I think, that has made me an empiricist, because I prefer a world that is reborn every moment, whole, to a past that resembles an abandoned factory where minutes sprout like weeds among the debris and the machines. I corresponded with Francisco Romero for years but I never dared to tell him that his humanism seemed crazy to me— the writing hand advances now from one side to the other and will keep going and is filling this great white space with signs— that everything existence assumes about the past is nothing but a delusion, beneficial in certain cases, I'll admit, but in the end a delusion. To me—oh how the boys would laugh if I said this in class—nothing exists but the present (not today, because "today" is too "broad" a concept for the idea I have of the present): my hand lifted in the air, now, that hangs at the height of the lamp (hanging, lamp, and height are three separate presents, each absolute, and only laziness makes me pull them together into a single sentence), and the room to one side, the bookcase that is behind me is nothing more than a delusion. It is my philosophy. It would be dishonest to explain it systematically. What's more, for me there is no relationship of cause and effect (there is nothing more than a whole universe that plunges, whole, into nothingness and then reappears, plunges, whole again, and reappears infinitely), and it is the cause and effect relationship that serves as the skeleton for all philosophic discourse, including those who propose to negate the relationship of cause and effect. Cicero, Saint Thomas, Kant, and Hegel, that pretentious Frenchman who went to Holland to look for the "cogito," are nothing more to me than sparkling specters whom I consider so little that they can't scare me. Sometimes I sense in a smell unfurling before me the phantasmagoria of a past so vivid that for a moment it makes me waver. But then I reflect that I have done nothing more than sense a new smell, of such a particular type that it awakens sensations that evoke memories, but that are not memories themselves, simply because there is nothing to remember. The philosophy students know me for my love of grilled fish and white wine, for my affability and some rough and poorly made socks that my wife makes me wear all year round to stave off the cold.

A Historian's Insomnia

A small silver cup of *mate* comes and goes from my worktable. Sometimes the last one goes cold on the pedestal. My study is a knot of cool semidarkness, fortified by books against the summer that sparkles behind the orange curtains. My greedy eye incessantly retraces daguerreotypes of full-grown men and oil paintings representing soundless, immobile battles. The life of those multitudes, has it been richer or more raucous than this life of mine, which fades away as my body atrophies within these four walls? Sometimes, a perfect, unexpected fragment unfurls and expands beneath my eyes, a report from San Martín, a letter, happy diamonds from an epoch of sun and blood. Mostly, however, there is nothing to do but copy documents from the archives and cobble together evidence that will exchange one glory for another on the overcrowded horizon of death. And most of all, the tension of ensuring that this nightmare that has fanned out behind me—and why do I say behind?—doesn't evaporate and isn't erased.

I work deep into the night before heading to bed. Whatever pretext serves to delay each night a little more. But at last there are no more excuses and I am undressing slowly, I am putting on my pajamas, and I am laying myself out next to the bulk of breathing heat that is the sleeping body of my wife. The procession begins immediately, the mute creaking of insomnia, interwoven with changing forms that assault me and never leave until daybreak. Almost always, it ends with increasingly wild disintegration, whose final phases I forget most of the time, or perhaps I'm already asleep, or perhaps I believe that I'm already asleep, or perhaps I'm absorbed in a thought of which I'm not conscious, but that nevertheless I believe I understand. Yet, despite everything, none of these is the worst. Some nights it's not dreams that follow insomnia, but blind lucidity, an incandescent vigil, that is no sort of lucidity at all and a vigil for nothing. Having reached that point, I feel emptied of memories—I, for whom memory is the masculine arm that parts the waters and, at the same time, the turbulent river whose bottom keeps receding, even as one plunges deeper—and with nothing to think about. Then, in the lilac sky, the white pinpoint of the moon begins to rise slowly and sparkle against the metallic curtains.

The Septuagenarian Poet

I ate the foods of the world. My hand touched the stones of famous cities and my body, shriveled now but fit and feral, walked streets more numerous than the ripples in a river. What man have I not known? What book have I not read? What might there be in the warehouse of visible and invisible things that could still be sold to me as a novelty? In the mornings of the month of October, full of sunlight and pigeons, I contemplate the slow explosion of peach blossoms and I stroll leisurely along, enjoying good digestion and good respiration, the taste of coffee on my tongue and a lit cigarette between my fingers. I had to go through all of that, the long night of desire and possession, to get here.

My mind hammers strange iron verses. They echo in me as if for the first time. Beauty, which for Plato is reminiscence, for me, defenseless and free, is nothing but immediate reality. The same alliterative music makes me shudder again, each time, with resplendent delight. Coffee: a shadow compared to its aftertaste, with its perfumed heaviness now subtly radiating from the tip of my tongue. What saves us now, we old people, is to see the world burning behind us, seated on a blazing bed of ash. Upon that mattress I sit and contemplate my own shadow as the morning makes it slowly shrink away.

Today I hope that others enjoy the miracle of birth and the flavor of their first perfumed presentation to the world, or of the throngs of people at a party at night. To a blind man the sun is blacker than night, and the ideal birth is death. My light is unique. I cannot change it. And the smoke from my cigarette is bluer and more solid than a cluster of cities.

The Lookalike

A friend of mine, a writer, having discovered his wife was cheating on him with a bank employee (when usually it's the wives of bank employees who cheat on their spouses with writers), left his house one day and after wandering in the mountains for a while, working at a newspaper in Mendoza, *The Andes*, I think, and living off the beneficence of a wine merchant who supported poets and painters, disappeared completely, without dropping the smallest hint to me or to any of his friends about where he might be, until one morning in March when I was obliged to get up early (I live on the outskirts of the city, in the Colastiné Norte), when I opened the front door and suddenly found myself facing a man on horseback, who told me he was passing through the local post office and, when he mentioned he was headed in the direction of my house, had collected a letter for me that had been gathering dust at the post office for more than two months—it was airmail, because the fine paper envelope was bordered by red and blue stripes, and when I opened it I found that it held a postcard—Hans Memling's *Sybilla Sambetha*—on the back of which my friend, from Bruges, Belgium, had written to tell me that he was very well, that he felt 10 years younger, and that he lived with a tiny Japanese woman who never spoke a word and who had learned to brew *mate*.

People who don't live here can't imagine how hot it is, even in March, so that the sun at eight in the morning had already sucked the dew off the leaves hours ago, and its light now roasted my scalp as I waited for the bus, looking at the portrait of the Sybil Sambetha, so familiar to me, though it was the first time I had ever seen it, that the face it reminded me of, even though I couldn't recall exactly whose it was, grew within me from the wide and rigid stain of pink marbling, stretched even further because of her taught locks disappearing behind, gathered into a conical bun and covered by tulle falling in geometric pleats onto her shoulders, and because her dress, painted in a color I would call "oil," opened at her throat into a circular collar. The revelation of that memory, the identity of that face, was on the tip of my tongue, if you could call it that, and with ever more effort I tried to figure out who it was, I tried to force that memory from the black backdrop into the great spotlight of my mind, so that it would change from the type of memory that didn't need to be remembered into something palpable and real. I was still consumed with remembering when the bus arrived, half empty, slow, chromed, alone on the blue strip of asphalt, sparkling in the sun and full of the noise of metal and motors. I took out my ticket and was about to sit when suddenly I saw the Sybil, tranquil and alone, looking at me with her pensive little eyes from the back seat. The porous diagonal light of the sun fell on her face, so that the rosy, marble skin turned a resplendent gold. Her whole face was peppered with blackheads and pimples, some of them crowned with white jewels of pus. But the wide fore-head was the same, and her neck rose, free, from the round collar of a cotton dress printed with red and green flowers. I had seen her many times, the disfigured face, the black hair pulled back, taught, her gaze more placid and pensive than one hand hitting the other with a wet wisteria vine—seated on the bench, looking at the river from the door of her father's ranch, a fisherman whom I went to see from time to time to order a certain fish or a covey of wild ducks. I was about to show her the portrait, but I am a timid man, almost weak of character, and after all, what did it matter?

I've seen twins who look very much alike, but never as alike as *Sybilla Sambetha* and the girl from the coast. And yet, could there be two more different people? Nothing made me consider them so different as to see them looking so alike. For several days this likeness disquieted me and made me feel, by contrast, the reality of difference more than of similarity, because the reality of difference evidences the reality of uniqueness, what Marx mocked, and, melancholically, I thought much about the infinity of trees and of rocks, of faces, of birds, of excrements, of roots, each one unrepeatable and alone, unique; I experienced the clichéd impression of the ocean's infinite waves and the uncountable sands, of the past, the present, and the future which flow, depending on how you view them, in different directions and crash into each other, forming knots and collisions that we think we can decipher, and suddenly (it was noon and I was lying naked in the sun so that its light would scorch me, my eyes closed and my pores slowly opening with a secret creaking), euphorically, I longed to be a special type of minstrel, the minstrel of the visible world, the minstrel of all things, considering them one after the other, the minstrel of the two Sybils, to give each thing its place with an impartial voice that would equalize and reclaim them, to display in the middle of the day an entire world in which every paradise, every leaf of every paradise, every vein of every leaf of every paradise would be present, so that the entire world could contemplate itself in every part by the light of day and nothing would remain anonymous.

Argument over the Term "Zone"

Place: A restaurant called *El Dorado*, on the other side of the suspension bridge, over the costal road—more precisely, in a rough-edged tin cubicle, split in two by a wooden partition, with a wooden balcony overhanging the road and a back patio full of trees, separated from the river by a log railing. Beyond the railing the ground slopes into a ravine, and then the river. On the opposite bank, houses raised on wooden stilts expose their fragile façades to the water.

Time: One day in February of 1967, two in the afternoon.

Temperature: 99 degrees in the shade.

Protagonists: Lalo Lescano and Pigeon Garay. They were born on the same day in the same year, 1940, but while the members of the Garay family can claim to be descendants of the town's founder, Juan de Garay, the day that Lalo Lescano was born some local women had to take up a collection just to send his mother to the hospital as his father, a waiter in a restaurant, was several hours late getting home, and one can only suppose he spent them at the racetrack.

Setting: A farewell feast, because Garay is leaving in a few months for Europe, where he will be living for several years.

The argument begins when Garay says that he will miss this place and that a man should always be loyal to one region, one zone. Garay says this looking toward the water—they are seated at a table shaded from the sun by the trees—while, with his thumb and forefinger, he kneads a piece of newspaper that came wrapped around his grilled fish. Neither Lescano nor Garay are epicures by nature, but they go to this restaurant (though neither would admit it) because they know years ago it was a haunt for Higinio Gomez, Cesar Rey, Marcos Rosemberg, Jorge Washington Noriega, and others who passed for the literary vanguard of the city. When the piece of paper has been kneaded to death, Garay throws it in the direction of the river without bothering to see where it lands. Lescano follows the trajectory of the gray little ball with his eyes, and then says that there are no regions, or, at least, it's difficult to pin down the limits of a region. He explains: Where does the coast begin? Nowhere in particular. There is no precise point where you can say the coast begins. Let's take two regions, for example: the Pampa Gringa and the coast. They are imaginary regions. Is there a border between them, a real border besides the one that geography manuals have invented to manage things more easily? None. He, Lescano, is inclined to admit certain facts, that the earth is different, a different color, and that they grow wheat, flax, and alfalfa in the Pampa Gringa while, on the coast, it seems that the soil is better suited to rice, cotton, and tobacco. But, then, which is the exact point where people stop planting wheat and start planting cotton? Ethnically, the Pampa Gringa is made up primarily of foreigners, those being primarily Italians, while the coast is predominantly native-born families. But would you really say that there are no Italians on the coast and no natives in the Pampa Gringa? The Pampa Gringa is stronger economically, and we know, with precision, that the part of the coast closer to Cordoba is bordered by Entre Ríos and Corrientes. All of this suggests a principle of differentiation, I admit. But isn't it also possible to define the Pampa Gringa as the part of the coast that lies beyond Entre Ríos (the part of the coast farther from Entre Ríos, let's say), a part of the coast where, because of characteristics in the soil, they plant more wheat than cotton? I would admit that they belonged to different regions if there were a way of marking the borders with precision, but that possibility does not exist. Proximity to the river isn't a good argument, because there are parts of the coast that are nowhere near the river, and those are still called the coast. There is no precise limit: the final rice paddy is already inside the wheat fields, and vice versa. I'll give another example if you like: the city. Where does the city center end and the suburbs begin? The dividing line is conventional. Galvez Boulevard, let's say. But any one of us knows full well, because we were born here and we live here and we know the city by heart, that there are many things north of Galvez Boulevard that could easily be in the center: multi-story houses, apartment buildings, businesses, respectable families. And the city itself, where does it end? Not at the checkpoint, because the people who live beyond the checkpoint say, when you ask them where they live, that they live in the city. So there can't be zones. I don't understand, Lescano concludes, how you can be loyal to a region, when regions don't exist.

I disagree, says Garay.

Anonymous Biography

Sometimes we think about nuclear explosions or this used-up planet dangling in the black expanse because God is great, and a shudder runs over our entire body and makes us want to scream, but in a moment we forget and we go back to imagining all the things we could do if one day we received a laconic letter from California informing us that an unknown relative had just bequeathed us a million dollars. In winter we impatiently await the summer, but when we find ourselves at last beneath the January sun, bronzing slowly, doing nothing, we begin to feel as if our mind were circling around a retracted pinhole, a tiny whirlpool winding inward and downward, an implacable spiral. Then come the unchanging days: work, school for the kids, the possibility of a promotion or a subtle change of direction in our life that we discuss cautiously with our wife in bed, before we fall asleep, or maybe a new house, a memory, some party where the first few cups of alcohol excited us and made us say crazy things that puffed us up because everyone else thought they were funny. Our body changes. Nothing happens if we bathe in the morning, because we have to go immediately to the office and what's more we're still half asleep, but sometimes, later, home from work, having plunged into the bath because we will be going out to the movies with our wife or going for dinner at a friend's place, we remain awhile under the tepid water and then look attentively at our naked body in the bathroom mirror or in the one in the closet, as we dry off. All things considered, we keep ourselves up. One day when there was a protest we decided not to go to work and followed the bulletins on a transistor radio, arguing over them. We remember distinctly how we would get worked up, especially over a new guy, a young man whom we didn't much like because his yellow teeth had half rotted away, and how one day, all of a sudden, he disappeared without giving the least notice or saying goodbye to any of his friends. Now we don't even remember his name. Next year, if all goes well, we'll go to Brazil or to Punta del Este in Uruguay. When we are melancholy we take the car and drive alone in circles around the city—if we can, we even like to go out past the checkpoint and get into the countryside, and once we got all the way to Esperanza. It was a summer night and people were sitting on the sidewalks drinking beer in the bars spread out around the plaza. Coming home we saw how the moon bleached the endless, motionless fields of wheat so that they looked almost metallic. We sleep well and never dream. In another time, before we got married, we used to suffer bouts of insomnia and we would watch the green and red lines of a neon sign slip through the intermittent cracks in the blinds and project onto the white bedroom walls. Other than that, we've never had problems with our health, thank God, either because we don't smoke or just by chance, and we've managed to keep ourselves safe from the terrible things that happen to other people. When our wife is pregnant, we entertain ourselves, in the last month, by putting our ear against her belly to hear what is moving inside, the movement of the child that is beginning to prepare to break away and fall into this multiple marvel, the world. Instinctively we close our eyes, throbbing, terrified, because it seems that from one moment to the next we can hear, clearly, the roar of that terrible crash.

Hands and Planets

Barco's familiar and skillful fingers unscrewed the chrome top of the saltshaker, dumped the salt onto the tablecloth and then, under Tomatis' tranquil but astonished gaze, began to scatter it, his fingertips pressing onto the grains and turning slowly to fully spread out that little white mountain on the blue cloth. Barco's fingertips had an extraordinarily peculiar shape: they were oval and tapered—they looked like the classical representation of a teardrop. In the whole world there couldn't have been another pair of hands with fingertips like that, and Tomatis would have recognized them immediately from anywhere.

"Probably," said Barco, "in many of these grains of salt there are Ancient Greeces where Heraclitus is thinking that the events of the world are the product of a game of dice played by children."

"Probably," said Tomatis.

"Last night on television I saw the latest mission to the moon," said Barco. "No one cares about those missions to the moon anymore. The whole world is convinced that the moon is already a thing of the past, and that science fiction is becoming an anachronism. Fiction can't keep up with science anymore. Probably, in fifty years everyone will be a scientist, the way that nowadays everybody drives a car."

"Probably," said Tomatis, without taking his eyes off of Barco's fingers, which were now resting on the scattered salt and remained motionless.

"Something strange happened," Barco said. "Everything was going fine when they were showing the inside of the spaceship and the crew working on the screen. But suddenly they began showing pictures of the Earth as it got farther and farther away, getting smaller every minute, and then everyone watching the television in the bar stopped what they were doing, or started to sit up slowly in their chairs, or to strain their necks, all this trying to keep the Earth closer, contorting themselves to help the Earth stop in its tracks, like when you're bowling and you twist yourself around so that the ball will follow the imaginary path you've laid out for it, you know? We all tried to get this obscene distancing to stop, so that the Earth wouldn't be erased and disappear forever. I was frozen stiff. And when the voice of the narrator announced that the astronauts could still make out Mexico, we all felt a moment of relief and for a moment we all felt as if we were Mexican: Mexico was the final crest, the highest, mounted by the wave of nothingness that pushed up from behind, the wave of nothingness that, when we could no longer make out Mexico, flooded everything and left it smoother and more uniform than this wall here. Then we all felt sad and confused, a bit frightened, and I don't think we felt any better when the program about the mission to the moon ended and they cut to the live game at Chacarita Stadium. I'm convinced that last night we broke the identity barrier. Breaking the speed of light or the sound barrier is nothing compared to breaking the barrier of identity. We kept on being erased, until we totally disappeared. We thought that things would stop at some point before they got out of hand, at some point from which we could still make out Mexico, for example, but no, nothing like that, we totally disappeared. And I felt something even more vertiginous: sitting in the chair at the bar, the screen showed me how the Earth had been shrinking, that is, I, the chair, the bar, the screen and the earth on the screen, shrinking, how we were being squeezed by the fist of the cosmos that closed upon us, vertiginously, macerating our bodies and turning them into hardened lava. And I felt it so intensely that I closed my eyes and waited for the walls of the bar to start closing in, subtly, molding the four into a single wall with us inside, in an inconceivable contraction, until the whole Earth had shrunken to the size of little dice with which little children would play out the destiny of the world. Probably, these grilled fish the waiter is bringing are ours."

"Probably," said Tomatis, seeing Barco's familiar fingertips press into the salt and then lift to his thick lips, fingertips that, like no others in the world—and now also because of their flavor—made him think of the solid form of tears.

The Mourner

One rainy morning in November I slept in until after it was light. The murmur of the water was audible, both complex and monotonous—that's been said so many times of water! Greenish light came into the room through the blinds. I lay in bed with my eyes open, staring at the semidarkness that was growing ever weaker, but that gathered against the ceiling. The dream I'd just had remained in my mind, persistent, a dream in which I had seen my uncle Pedro, my mother's brother, who worked for a long time in the factory and then afterward struck out on his own and opened a bakery. My uncle had died the month before. In the dream he seemed to be mourning his own death.

Dreams scare me, and sleep even more so. Am I afraid of what I dream or am I simply afraid of dreaming? I was sad that morning, thinking about my uncle Pedro who ended up dying just as his bakery was starting to do all right, but then, fortunately, curiosity overcame my sadness and I began to meditate on the meaning of the dream until almost nine. All this time it rained without stopping, and the noise of the rain lulled me almost to sleep, so that now I'm not sure whether at times I didn't dream up the meaning of what I had dreamed. A female friend of mine, a school teacher who later married a professor of mathematics and moved to Peru, told me that she had always dreamed of mourning over her own coffin. That she saw herself dead and mourned. Do we always mourn for ourselves when we mourn in dreams? Only the mourner knows that. Looking into this fount of tears is a difficult task, and curiosity's quiet gaze cannot see so deep. To see that pain, we have to be inside it. But what is even more surprising is that he who mourns himself, the one who sees his cadaver or offers condolences to himself over his own death, stands at such a singular point in the great plain of pain that his cry is at the same time a memory and an anticipation. In the great plains the horizon is always a circle, identical, empty and monotonous.

Regarding Autumn Siestas

The sun in April doesn't sink, it slims. We go out walking after dinner, avoiding the cold shade and stopping every once in a while to look at a yellowing frond, the ornamentation on a façade. We argue over sex and politics. For me, they are siestas full of statues and delicate sun; after several blocks, my temples begin to throb. We pass through the Plaza de las Palomas, head to the promenade, lean over the rail, and look at the river. As I see it, it is at that hour that cities flatten and stretch out. It has seemed to me, at times, that I know everything about statues, about the urine that disfigures and stains them, about the old houses that bear witness to more perfect lives.

Even finer, the dusty sunlight—at a certain hour—is smooth and omnipresent. We sit on a wooden bench, on powdered brick paths, to warm our heads. Suddenly we are silent. What we call the murmur, the soft sound of years of life, the sound of what we remember, is passing by, bit by bit, until it falls utterly silent. Then we begin to hear sounds outside: a car, far off, the shouts of two boys calling to one another beyond the park and the rotunda of the promenade, even the clicks of women's heels as they tap against the powdered brick. I know of nothing more real. Within my heart—could you call it that?—the empty echo of those whispers resounds. I've surprised myself in those moments, asking with a sudden dread "Who am I and what am I doing here?"

Afterward, when we are walking again and we go into the first bar, the feeling disappears, I have worked out a theory that the April sun flowing slowly downward onto the city is unhealthy, and that its effects are like those of marijuana, but more diffuse.

Friends

Angel Leto, an old friend of Barco and Tomatis's whom they hadn't heard from in years, was alone in a house waiting for the appointed moment to kill a man. It was a winter morning, green and rainy, and Leto, who had just gotten up, came from the kitchen through the semidarkness of the hallway into the light of the living room, carrying with him a cup of coffee. If he followed through with the plan, by the next day at half past eight in the morning the man would already be dead and Leto would be back in the house where Tomatis's books were carefully lined up on the bookshelf, gathering dust while their owner spent the summer in Europe.

It was, in fact, Tomatis's apartment, to which Barco had given him the keys two days earlier. Barco had found Leto in his kitchen, on another rainy morning, and had given him the keys, neither put out nor surprised even though it had been nearly eight years since the last time he had seen him. And, as Leto thought that very night, in bed, as he flipped through Tomatis's originals with pleasure and credulity, smoking a cigarette by lamplight against the monotonous background of the June rain that enveloped the night like a cocoon, if Barco didn't yet know exactly what he was up to in the city, within two or three days, if he read the papers, he would be sure to figure it out.

And now Leto, in his second morning at Tomatis's place, walked to the living room from the kitchen, through the dark hall, with the white cup on the white saucer balanced on the palm of his hand.

He sat down, placing the cup carefully on the table, and set about reading one of Tomatis's manuscripts held in a green folder upon which Tomatis had printed, in red ink, a word Leto didn't know: PARANATELLON. On the first page inside the folder there were three words printed all in capital letters, one after the other, separated by several spaces, in the following order:

PARANATELLON

PARANATELLERS

OR

PARNASUS

And farther down an inscription in lowercase:

An annotated anthology of the coast

A bit later, when the last sip of coffee at the bottom of the cup had gone cold, Leto lifted his eyes from the typed pages, and, leaning the nape of his neck on the backrest of the chair and contemplating the ceiling, he began to think of the man he was going to kill. The man who had been the object of his every action these past several months could not hold his attention for long, because his thoughts soon wandered to considering death in general. His first thought was that, for all that he might riddle this man's body with bullets, as he fully intended to do, *he would never manage to completely rid the world of him.* The man deserved to die: he was a union leader who had betrayed his class and whom Leto's group held responsible for several assassinations. But, thought Leto, as if his ideas emanated from the grayish emptiness that extended between the lamp and the ceiling, killing him would only take him out of immediate action, not out of reality.

And Leto remembered when he was eighteen and a friend of his age had died after an operation. Now that he was thirty-three, it seemed that, after fifteen years, time had lost its fearsome character and his dead friend remained as present in the world as he himself, independent from his memories and authority. *What comes into the world,* Leto thought, *can never go out again.* The infinitude of stars would remain, whether they liked it or not, wandering around with us inside them. And, like a bird that eats its own eggs, time went on erasing events as they unfolded, leaving nothing to human life but its indeterminate presence, a kind of clot of solidarity that kept reducing and encrusting itself in some imprecise point in the infinite, and from which every individual, as a just consequence of his mortal condition, formed a part. This clot, thought Leto, was of a singular quality: it could never be erased. Its presence had produced an irreversible alteration, redeeming the universe from pure ostentation; after its appearance, nothing would continue as before, and death—the death of his friend, the death of the man he was going to kill, his own death—was an insignificant accident.

No one can be killed, Leto thought, *except one's friends, but one cannot even kill them, because it is impossible to kill what is immortal.*

Beaches

The riverbanks sparkle, slowly, like signals: they ripple. The ocean is one and the same, always. Only its borders move, in place, and when one edge advances, it is the entire ocean advancing. We stand before the sea so that it can contemplate us. But we are always on one side of the river as it passes us without regard, disdainful. Its beaches are an immobile caravan of umbrellas—red ones, blue, orange with white stripes, green, spotted. The yellow sand splays out before the caramel-colored water in a weak semicircle. Burned bodies pass by, running along the border of the water, and on the shore they form the tri-colored fringe of a most unusual rainbow: the yellow border of the sand, the tawny water, and the transparent strip, between the two, of water kicked up by the constant drum of feet that convulse the shore. Gazing after the running feet, not considering their prior upheavals that have already been erased, always keeping your eyes locked on the feet hitting the water, you can perceive the transparent, whitish fringe, like an imaginary dotted line, between the sand and the river. If this description seems overwrought, just remember that more stable fringes, so to speak, like the white and red fringes of umbrellas are also, if you will, in essence, imaginary and interrupted borders.

Now we have returned from the beach and it is two-thirty in the afternoon. We are sprawled out on the bed, in a cool white room protected by dark curtains; there is another body, also naked, next to our own. To that empty cavern comes no more than the memory, and that only for a moment, of overlapping shores, of immobile paths, white and deserted. Now we see trees with leaves covered in a white powder that resembles volcanic ash. Now we see nothing. We feel that the other body is hot, thick, and burnt. We imagine that our own must be, too. We weave together in an intermittent struggle, interspersed with moments of complete immobility, in which we see our shaggy hair, our knees, our genitals, which fit together, which complement each other, our feet which lie placid, gnarled, isolated at the far end of the bed; we compare the burnt parts of our bodies with the white ones, in the places where we usually wear our bathing suits. Afterward we tangle ourselves into the final battle. We had touched the furthest point, the muddy bottom of the river, passed the riverbed and arrived in a translucent zone beyond the convulsed, blinding bottom, a point full of light like the very center of a diamond. That light was so intense that nothing could be seen, not even the light itself. In that struggle we came back up, dense and spinning, like the body of a drowned man, toward the confused darkness of the bottom where we engaged in combat. Further up the surface of the world remains, with the beaches, the pathways, the crowds, the city, the dark room where our bodies, now, are sprawled out immobile on the bed, looking at the ceiling. At noon we had stopped on the shore, trying to hear the multiple murmurs of the water, the polyrhythm and polyphony at the heart of it's enduring monotony. We could make out nothing in that murmur except that it sounded a bit unsettling to us because we could make out nothing in it. At the same moment, on the other side of the border, a stingray, clotted with nerves and cartilage, stretching out to enjoy the heat of the shallower water close to shore, believes all of a sudden it feels, in the great confusion of its subcutaneous sensations, a monotonous murmur emanating from the beach, a murmur which it does not realize is composed of many voices: the song of the world.

Gandia's Bar

Don't be fooled: the news that came out in the paper last week, in the police blotter, which says very clearly that the owner of a bar, named Gandia, was arrested, gives a false impression of the person in question. It's true that, as it appears, he played cards for money behind the bar, and that in the rooms out back a girl from the neighborhood, one of the poorest in the city, received her clientele, from which Gandia made a small commission. But don't be fooled, don't be put off: It's not Gandia that news is about, it's someone else, someone I've met.

That they would have put him in jail makes me smile. What's more, it's not the first time this has happened. In this slum, Gandia's bar is the hub of perdition, the vicinity of vice. It is an obligatory stop for any backsliding prole. And its owner, Gandia, son of a laborer or a farmer—I don't really know—has rough, callused hands, weighs over 200 pounds and is always dirty and poorly shaven. He is one of those men whose sullenness is too childish to be offensive, frightening, or even convincing. One can see from afar that Gandia is tangled up in himself, perpetually absorbed in internal discord, for reasons surely even he doesn't know, and what appears to others is the harshness radiating from that derangement, like that man whom one sometimes encounters fruitlessly trying to screw in, for hours, the same microscopic little screw, and who greets one in a huff.

Gandia is a great card player. He's a special card player, though: he cheats. Everyone in the world has discovered this trait, and yet no one has stopped playing cards with him. This is because Gandia, unlike other card players, whether they are cheaters or not, cheats and *still manages to lose*. He loses: an incontestable fact that all his patrons know. What's more, they have seen players who, in the midst of a hand, have had the wisdom to consider Gandia's tricks as a rational part of the game, which gives an idea of regularity and defined and cognoscible character to his cheating. Rarely has Gandia won a hand. With a new player when he's at his best, the first time, because the second time the new player will have already adapted himself to the rules of the game as it is played at Gandia's bar.

I don't think that it makes any sense to form a moral judgment in Gandia's case. There's a more pertinent explanation and I think I can supply it: Gandia cheats out of courtesy. Destined to lose, Gandia diminishes the effect of his deep-seated inclination by cheating. It's a courtesy to himself in the first place, since cheating gives his existence, otherwise purely linear, like a pebble falling from a vacuum into an abyss, the illusion of decline; for the other players, too, ridding them, through his tricks, of their scruples; and lastly, a sublime courtesy for the world outside, so mute and so fine, to supply it with, at his expense, a dramatic depth.

But the news that they had taken him into custody last week makes me smile. Don't get worked up about it.

White Hot

In this family, my brother would say whenever there was some kind of argument, the sane ones are traitors. He died last week in the mental hospital. He had spent the last twenty years of his life in there: I remember when I was little, we went to see him every Sunday with a package of sponge cake and oranges, and that sometimes he wouldn't deign to receive us. Sometimes a male nurse would come to let us know that my brother was in no mood for visitors, and then we would head out along the dirt road toward the streetcar stop, more confused or humiliated than saddened, in the sunny hours of the Sunday siesta.

As I found out later from my mother, my brother's illness had begun one very dry summer: the city, the surrounding countryside and the rivers were all baking slowly in the white January sun. You could barely step out onto the street or look in the direction of the sun. The city was practically empty; you could walk the streets for hours and not bump into anyone. The branches of the trees were gray and scorched, and the light beat down, bright, somewhat ashen, upon the patios.

One day that summer, my brother, who was eighteen then and about to go to work on the railway like my father, refused to come out of his room for two days, claiming that just outside there was a huge diamond burning out his sight. Quite affably, as if he were speaking with a child, he explained to my father from the far side of the bolted door how, on the street the day before, on Western

Avenue, in front of the General Store, he had seen a long diagonal line that stretched from a man's eyes to one of the facets of the diamond, his sight-line, burn in a instant from one end to the other like a fuse going off. He said that he had seen the man run off with his eyelashes singed. On the second day when my father and other family members decided at last to force the door open, they found my brother sitting calmly in bed, one leg bent and the other crossed over the knee of the first—a detail which, for whatever reason, made my mother smile every time she told me the story.

When they found him on the bed, my brother's eyes were shut tight, and he never really opened them again. We had to bring him to doctors, to treatments, and eventually to a psychiatrist as if he were a blind man, guiding him through that darkness of his own making with which he protected the integrity of his sight. And when, after months, after years of being shut up in the insane asylum, he opened his eyes one day, he had the courtesy to explain to a doctor, who, in turn, explained to us, smirking ironically beneath his neatly trimmed mustache, that he would open his eyes *metaphorically*, in appearance only, that, during the years he had spent with his eyes closed, he had been constructing, just behind the eyes themselves, a fixed gaze, inalterable even in the face of fire, to confront that terrible light. In highly complex and scientific terminology, the doctor told us, my brother had explained his methods. The terms I emphasize here belong to his scientific lexicon: with his eyes closed he had been absorbing particles of light from the outside whose *explosive shock* would be diminished as they penetrated through the filter of his eyelids, and which accumulated behind his eyes and fortified his new *visual apparatus*. My brother had followed, according to his own expression, the laws of that *rigorous science,* homeopathy.

I leave it to the specialists among my readers to form their own opinion about my brother's scientific and technological wherewithal. All I can say is that last week, hours after having passed on to the next world, his eyes were still open—he remained in that condition until one of my uncles, bothered perhaps by the scientific triumph that had overcome sight, decided to place a one peso coin on each eyelid to keep them shut.

A Change of Residence

A couple years ago I changed my residence and I changed my name. Politics had a hand in it—in Buenos Aires the police noticed me during a rally and since, despite my advanced ideas, I couldn't muster any compelling evidence to prove I wasn't part of some clandestine organization, I felt it was best to make a change of residence and disappear for a while. So I got on the bus and came to this city where everything bakes in the summer on the banks of the great river.

There's nothing like travel to encourage introspection. In the bus's mobile, noisy night, the traveler's eye stays open, insomniac, or alert, more accurately, to the music of the world. It was on the bus, really, where the idea to supplant my simple act of self-defense with a radical change of identity first, unexpectedly, feverishly, occurred to me. I would start another life with another name, another profession, another appearance, another destiny. I would emerge, with five or six vigorous strokes, from the sea of my past onto a virgin shore. With no family, with no friends, with no job, with no *Piccolo mondo antico* whose womb I could pickle in, the future seemed smooth and luminous, and tender above all, like a newborn babe. I set up in a guesthouse, forged my documents, transformed myself physically and took a job as a door-to-door book salesman. The newspapers gave me up for dead. It was said that the secret police were after me. But the reigning terror let nothing appear on the surface except in the form of ambiguous allusions.

All of this happened about two years back. In the second or third month of my new existence, realizing that my habits hadn't changed much, I decided to modify my tastes and customs systematically. I stopped smoking. I had always hated kidney beans and fatty meat, so I started eating them every day until they became my favorite foods. I decided to write with my left hand, and introduced major changes into my most deeply held convictions. In this way I utterly changed my personality within a year. I seemed to be, you might say, a different man.

I say "I seemed to be," as you can see, and not "I was." In retrospect I now realize that there was a sort of blockage in my life, of which I was barely conscious, inciting me to change: the sensation that I was going around in a circle, never moving forward, of being always a little too far from or close to things, of failing to fit into any definition, of never knowing for certain whether I was dreaming or awake, of not knowing how to choose between the well defined options which others presented to me. For years it had seemed to me that this ineptitude was mine alone, subjective, that my personal history had unfolded so as to imprison me within it, practically incapable of decision, and that others, whom I perceived from the outside, did not experience, in this world, the smallest inconvenience. Nevertheless, within two years my husky smoker's voice disappeared, along with my Buenos Aires accent, but the ancient reservoir that lies low and sometimes trembles, heavy, down below, sending up signs of life, reminds me that, though I have chosen a convenient mask, we humans, whatever the color of our destiny, will never be adequate to our circumstances, or, frankly, to the world.

Veiled

A furniture salesman who had just purchased a second-hand armchair discovered that, in the hollow part of the backrest, one of the former owners had hidden a diary. For some reason—death, forgetfulness, abandonment, seizure—the diary had remained there, and the salesman, an expert in furniture construction, had come upon it accidentally as he tapped the back of the armchair to test its sturdiness. That day he stayed late in the store stacked full of beds, chairs, tables, and dressers, hunched over his desk in the back office reading the diary by lamplight. Day by day, the diary revealed the emotional problems of its author, and the salesman, who was an intelligent and sensible man, understood at once that the woman had been hiding her true nature, and that by some incomprehensible twist of fate he now knew her far better than any of the people who had lived alongside her and whom she mentioned in the diary.

The salesman sat thinking. For a while the idea that someone could keep something hidden in her house, something veiled from the world—a diary or whatever it might be—seemed strange to him, almost impossible, until a few minutes later, at the moment he stood up and began to tidy his desk before heading home, he noted, with no little astonishment, that he himself had, in some places, hidden things the rest of the world knew nothing about. In his house, for example, in the attic, in a tin box buried among old magazines and useless junk, the salesman had hidden a roll of bills that thickened from time to time, and whose existence was unknown even to his wife and children. The salesman could not say precisely why he was saving that money, but little by little it had been adding to the unpleasant certainty that *his whole life* was defined not by the quotidian activities he performed by the light of day, but by that roll of bills crumbling in the attic; and that undoubtedly all of his actions, at their base, were aimed at adding another bill every once in a while to that crumbling roll.

As he turned on the neon sign, filling the black air over the pavement with a violet light, the salesman was seized with another memory: he had been looking for a pencil sharpener in his eldest son's room when he stumbled upon a series of pornographic pictures his son had hidden in a dresser drawer. The salesman had put back the pictures immediately, less from embarrassment than from the fear that his son would think he was in the habit of snooping.

During dinner, the salesman observed his wife; for the first time in thirty years it occurred to him that she might also be keeping something hidden, something so personal and so deeply buried that, even if she wanted to, even under torture, she could not have confessed it. The salesman felt a sort of vertigo. It wasn't some banal fear of being betrayed or swindled that made his head spin as if he were drunk, but the certainty that, just as he stood at the brink of old age, he might find himself compelled to modify the most elemental notions of his life. Or what he had called his life: because his life, his real life, according to his new intuition, turned out to be in another place, in the darkness, veiled from events, and that life seemed more remote to him than the very outskirts of the universe.

The Mirror

For the boys at the office it's already completely natural, and almost all of them think of me as a good coworker. They even look out for me, and there is a tacit understanding between us whereby they accept me and I keep my private life out of the office, even though this divides my life in two. They consider me cultured, tasteful, delicate. It is difficult for a person like me to make it into his forties, I realize, and although they tolerate my idiosyncrasy, I feel that the time for revelries has ended and that maturity has come at quite a cost.

When book vendors come to the office, the boys always consult me before buying a set. I recommend Huxley (Aldous), Mauriac, Shakespeare, firstly because anyone can enjoy Shakespeare, and moreover because Shakespeare is such a well-respected author that someone might get offended if I didn't recommend buying his complete works. I never recommend Oscar Wilde or André Gide so as not to arouse suspicion, but I myself read them with an enthusiastic sarcasm, I brandish them in silence as evidence, alone, against no one, in our ancient house in the south where my mother and sister, old and deaf, move about in the evening shouting and almost swimming in the violet light that filters through the blinds. Since my room is the one at the end of the hall and I am the one supporting the family, on the days I don't stay out drinking wine until the last bars have closed in the wee hours of the morning, I receive "visitors." Sometimes, in the past few years, I've been obligated to pay, or at least provide a little gift.

It's just that there is a high price to seeing oneself in such bright light, a price that cannot be reckoned in cash or in kind. The others turn into me, and I am the others, so that I get back all that I give. To make the world in my image, I have had to turn myself into the world, and I spread myself out like it, offered up, open. I pass over the world along with everyone who passes over me. In the great mirror of love, the world and I regard each other, surprised, each in the guise of the other, attempting to read into that manifold inversion as into an impossible palimpsest.

My Name is Pigeon Garay

My name is Pigeon Garay. I've lived in Paris for five years (Hôtel Minerve, 13, rue des Écoles, 5eme). Last year, in July, Carlos Tomatis dropped by for a visit. He was fatter than ever, nearly 200 pounds I'd guess, smoking cigarettes as he has been doing for the past seven or eight years, and we talked in my room, sitting before the window with the lights off, until dawn. I still remember the complex, rhythmic sound of his breathing emerging from the darkness as the temperature of our dialogue began to rise.

Two or three days later he went to London, leaving me to steep in an atmosphere of memories part-rancid, part-renewed, part-dead. There was something in that spider web of memories that recalled a living thing, the dying cub that trembles a bit, still warm, when one gently pokes it to see if it has died, with the tip of a stick or a finger. Afterward the thing stopped flowing and the animal went rigid, dead, made only of edges and cartilage.

My name, I say, is Pigeon Garay. *So to speak.*

Memories

Here you have me practically losing my voice and full of memories. They must be governed by some law; that is certain. But to discover that law it is necessary to empty oneself of them, to turn oneself inside-out like a glove. Everyone knows, anyway, that they obey no chronology. The philosophical prison we all carry within us has unleashed an assault onto our memories, decreeing unto them the fiction of chronology. And yet they continue, obstinately, to be our only freedom.

Let them at least become an obsession. Then they would obey a sort of law of exceptions, strict and absolute. Someone called them "incessant." With a regularity all their own, certain memories of the smallest incidents, without any apparent narrative content, return again and again to our consciousness, neutral and monotonous, until, having returned so often, our consciousness invests them with feelings and categorizes them: just as when a stray dog passes by to contemplate us silently, every day, in front of our door, we end up giving him a name.

A narrative could be structured simply by juxtaposing memories. It would just need a reader without illusions. A reader who, having read so many realist narratives that tell a story from beginning to end as if their authors possessed the laws of memory and of existence, aspired to something a bit more real. This new narrative, based purely on a foundation of memories, would have no beginning or end. It would be more of a circular narrative, and the position of the narrator would be like that of a boy who, riding a horse on a merry-go-round, tries at each pass to snatch a steel loop from the ring. It takes luck, skill, and continual adjustments of position, and having them all one would still come up most of the time empty handed.

There are many types of memories. Generalized memories, for example. During my childhood, during our summer siestas, my uncles would drive over from the neighboring village and the car's chrome radiator, glittering in the sunlight, would be full of yellow butterflies smashed into the metal vents. The image that remains with me is not of any particular event. It is an abridgement, almost an abstraction, of all the times I saw radiators full of butterflies. And yet it is a memory.

There are also immediate memories: we are bringing a cup of tea to our lips when we remember, even before the cup reaches its destination, the previous moment when we lifted it noiselessly from the table. And I would even venture to say that there is also a category we could call simultaneous memories, which consist of remembering the instant we are living in the same instant we live it; that is, we remember the taste of this tea and no other, in the same moment we are drinking it.

There are intermittent memories, which flicker periodically like lighthouses. Distant memories with which we remember, or think we remember, the memories of others. And also memories of memories, in which we remember remembering, or which present us with the memory of a moment when we had remembered something intensely. As you can see, remembering is complex stuff. Memory itself is not sufficient to grasp it. Voluntarily or involuntarily, our memory cannot control the act of remembering; it is more accurately a servant to it. Our memories are not, as empiricists claim, purely illusions: but nevertheless an ontological scandal separates us from them, constant and continual and stronger than any effort we can exert to construct our lives like a narrative. That is why, from another point of view, we could consider our memories a region even more remote than the whole world outside ourselves.

The Traveler

He broke the watch   the glass that protected the great face
whose Roman numerals ended in florid filigrees   delicate   he
scattered the pieces onto the smoking heap of ash that two nights
ago had been a flickering fire he himself had set

He had squatted for a moment   utterly absorbed in the childish task of brushing all the gray, caked-on lumps of soot from the
glass   afterward he paused and gazed at his surroundings

It continued to drizzle   slowly impalpably   condensing   so
that it looked more and more like mist   expanding toward the
great circular horizon

His face remained firmer and calmer than if he had raised it to see
the time on Big Ben

He was so accustomed to that plain which seemed to retreat before
him even as he advanced that he felt for a moment the illusion of
not having progressed at all   he had become so familiar with
it and at the same time had always thought of himself as such a
genteel and resigned sort of fellow   that the notion of wandering
around in it for the past five days   his horse had tripped in a
ditch   cracking one of its front hooves   the notion of having

walked around in circles without being able to find any point of reference a ranch a tree   or any possibility of using the stars to guide him since it had not let up raining for more than a few hours in the whole five days and even when it had the sky had never fully cleared   the notion of being lost on the plain   without a thing to eat without speaking anything but English without seeing another living thing besides some birds   black stiff high   in the air   migrating   they didn't seem to elicit any emotion from him   serene confirmation   cold desperation   perplexity

The moment before he broke the watch his perplexity had grown somewhat   discovering that after having walked for two days straight and stopping only once in a while to catch his breath   he had arrived once more at the place where a brief respite from the rain had allowed him to light a weak fire in the hope that someone would notice its glow   the perplexity grew somewhat settling in his face in the form of a wry smile

Nobody had seen a thing   not the fire he had lit nor the other fires   the ruddy face with bluish bags under the eyes   the red hair surrounding his large balding forehead and pate   the unrelenting water makes them glisten

Again he has come to the place where he lit the fire   he removed the watch from his pack   broke it   scattered the little shards of glass onto the ash heap   squatting

He stopped and gazed toward the horizon   *el pajonal*   he didn't know the straw was called that   it extended all the way to the uniform horizon   monotonously

He was up to his hips in it   straw

Sometimes   there were little clearings between the tufts of
grass   a man could lie down there and disappear   one had
to be there to know such clearings existed

When he advanced the blades of grass whipped open and then
closed behind him   he stopped   turned around   not even
a trace of his passage   he was going in circles and couldn't tell
the difference   not at all   his language his memory said I have
gone in circles   I have gone in circles I wasn't always looking
this way

He can't detect the smallest difference

It's precisely the same   the rain is denser or more transparent closer or farther away from the horizon   the gray
sky   below   the straw   *el pajonal*   he didn't know it
was called that   to the horizon   gray uniform monotonous

Reasonably and gracefully I accept   I have gone in circles   I'm
facing the other direction   Now I'm calling out again   I'm
in the same place again   I think   I persevere   Jeremy
Blackwood in the name of the company   establishes the cardinal
directions   I'll find the salting room

He looked at the ash heap   the broken watch   scattering he
continued to walk

He walked some incalculable interval

blackness more even than the straw and denser than the
rain   whipped by the supple blades of grass   immersed to the
hips   it rang in his mind in his memory   for hours   even

if it paused for a moment it did not crack   He could not filter
the silence

A dry snap ending in a sort of slipping   snapping back in place
the blades of grass unleashed   that   noise and made it swaying   and resounding

He awoke

Everything remained there   identical   severe   implacable   the rain the sky the horizon the straw

I know I've gone forward   the company from London   he
knew he was walking and advancing   I see   at dawn a
point identical to the rest   an identical point   but not the
same   I'm sure   it is my own word   against the rain the
sky the horizon the straw

He pants

Everything is wet   the leather sack   twisted stuck to his
body   the water   dripping   over his face   his carrot-red
locks   darkly blazing

He walked all day   I'm going to stop when the water stops   stopping only to catch his breath   the night came and the mist

He stopped

He toppled forward   onto the straw blades that opened and
closed like a whip

He remained sleeping   still

At dawn his dreams unfurled   a phosphorescent screen   he saw London   floating   illuminated like a transparent cathedral   London   red bricks   the sound of carriages resounding on the pavement   gossips calling out from window to window   markets   short pyramids of tomatoes   fish laid out smooth and open like women   live shrimps dragging themselves across the fishmonger's counter   lewd red beefsteak dismembered   prostitutes flashing their sin-stained tits   little boys running among the merchants   music from taverns and from the blind beggars rising above the throng

He awoke immobilized   his face squashed against the straw moved a bit   his eyes still closed   his smile shattered by his position and the shivering

I will get to the salting house because the company has chosen me   dignified honored predestined   Jeremy Blackwood redheaded and well bred with the reasoning and the memory of his station   to defeat   the temptation of the identical of the immobile

Blessed be London

Blessed be the throng that walks its benevolent pavements

Blessed be the light that shines from the windows of its houses

Blessed be the noise and the color of the cities

Jeremy sat   slowly   he kept his eyes open for a moment   proud

He lowers his head and sees again   the blackened ash heap   the
scattered shards of glass the broken open watch   the great face
whose Roman numerals ended in florid filigrees   delicate

Glory

To English travelers and more than anything

Glory

To Jeremy Blackwood who left not a trace of his journey

Abroad

Nothingness doesn't occupy my thoughts so much as my life, I read, some days ago, in a letter from Pigeon Garay. I don't give it the least thought all day; and I spend all night having dirty dreams. It must be because nothingness is a certainty, and there is a race of men, to which, presumably, I must belong, who only dance to the music of the uncertain.

That's the kind of thing that, occasionally, from abroad, I receive from Pigeon Garay. Or this: "Living abroad doesn't leave a trace, only memories. Often memories live outside us: a Technicolor film for which we are the screen. When the projection ends, darkness overcomes us again. Traces, on the other hand, which come from deeper, are the mark that accompanies us, deforms us and molds our face, like a punch molds a boxer's nose. One is always traveling while abroad. Children don't travel, they just expand their native country."

Another of his letters brought the following reflection: Garlic and the summer are two traces that always come to me from far away. Being foreign is a complex, useless mechanism that has taken garlic and the summer from me. When I find garlic and the summer again, foreignness demonstrates their unreality. I am trying to tell you that being foreign—that is, my life for the past six years—is a moronic circle, or perhaps a spiral, that pulls me around, again and again, level with the center, but a bit further away each time.

Re-reading this, I can confirm as usual that I have left the essential thing unsaid.

Or even: Blessed are those who stay behind, Tomatis, blessed are those who stay behind. Traveling so much, your footprints overlap, your traces are submerged or washed away and, at any rate, if you should ever come back, it comes with you, intangible, that foreignness, and seeps into the very place where you were born.

The Scattering

The people of my generation scatter, in exile. From the living branch of our youth there remain no more than two or three pale petals. Death, politics, marriage, travels have been silently separating us, prisons, possessions, oceans. Years ago, in the beginning, we met in blossoming patios and conversed until daybreak. We walked slowly around the city, from the illuminated streets of the center to the dark river, shrouded in the silence of sleeping neighborhoods, on the cool café sidewalks, in the paradise of our natal homes. We smoked tranquilly beneath the moon.

Of that past life, nothing remains but news or memories. But all of that is something compared with what has happened to those who have not scattered. Among them the exile is even greater. Each one has been immersing himself deeper into his own ocean of hardened lava, and when they imitate conversation, anyone can see that it is nothing more than noises, with no music or meaning. They have all turned their eyes inward, but those eyes see nothing more than a sea of minerals, smooth and gray, refracting every resolution. And if you can look into their pupils, which rarely happens, you would catch a glimpse of a desert compared to which the Sahara would doubtless acquire all the attributes of the Promised Land.

The Body

The body sends messages saying "don't forget, you up there." It throbs dully. Death, an elegant exit to such indecisive precariousness, approaches, coming from the very beginning by its own road, until it arrives, so to speak, out into the open. It keeps rising despite every obstacle or interruption.

The problem, Barco kept telling himself, was not in trying not to die, but in maintaining some equilibrium between what lay above and below, chance and its opposites. The body is chance. Its opposites vary historically—if not, really, ideologically.

Today I do not have the strength, truly; no strength. Not even that nourishing strength we call the power of seduction. The absence of hunger is morally wrong, they claim, in this century of gluttons. Do you see what I mean when I say that the opposites of chance vary historically? Illness, fatigue, failure of will: you have proven wisely the durability of chance against the dictatorship of insatiable hunger.

On Dry Shore

The day after acing his geometry exam, Tomatis convinced his father to renew his membership card at the Boating Club and spent the whole afternoon in the office going through the paperwork to reissue it. It was sitting in a cubicle while he waited for the new card that he conceived of the idea of the message, and when they gave him the card he went down to the bar and called Barco on the phone. Barco liked the idea. He said that he had sealing wax—because they would have to seal the top of the bottle—and that they should meet up that very night to discuss the contents of the message. So it was that, at around nine when it began to get dark, Tomatis heard Barco's voice from his room as Barco spoke with his father in the kitchen, followed by his footsteps coming up the stairs onto the landing. The window to Tomatis' room was open, and having entered without so much as a hello, Barco poked his head outside and said something about the starry sky. He undid the top two buttons of his shirt and began to wave it against his chest to dry his sweat. From the window Tomatis hollered to his mother to make them some sangria, because the whole house had been inclined to grant his every wish since the day before when, with his geometry exam, he had finished his degree. While they waited for the sangria, Barco helped him hang, on the yellow wall, over the couch, to one side of the bookshelf, a copy of Van Gogh's *Wheat Field with Crows* that Tomatis had gotten framed in a picture shop that morning.

They argued over the text of the message for more than two hours, drinking the sangria that Barco continually stirred with a spoon so that the sugar in it wouldn't settle and the ice tinkling against the inside of the frosty pitcher would melt faster. The idea of writing the message in verse, suggested by Tomatis, was rejected instantly.

"They might think we actually talked like that," Barco objected.

Immediately they began to throw out ideas: a summary of the city's history, or perhaps a catalogue of inventions of the era, or, better yet, a brief biography of Carlos Tomatis and Horacio Barco, or even a deliberately false description of the human body to provoke an erroneous theory of evolution. They were tempted for a moment by the last option and laughed about it until they were both in stitches, roaring so loudly that Tomatis's father, who had gone to bed some time earlier, scolded them from the darkness below to keep it down. Then Barco remarked that the inclination to humor always spoiled things, and that, in the end, the contents of the message didn't matter—the important thing was the message itself, because the value of a message lay not in what it said, but in its ability to reveal the existence of men disposed to writing messages. He said that if the contents of a message were so important, it wasn't a message at all but simply information.

"The best thing a message can say," said Barco, "is just *message*. So even when everything would seem to indicate we should write *HELP!*, I'd suggest that we write *this is a message*, or just *message*, short and sweet."

Tomatis considered this a moment and at last agreed, only to encounter another question: who would write the word?

"Keeping in mind," said Barco, "that the idea was yours and that there's reason to believe that in time you'll become a professional writer, I propose the writing of the text should fall to you." That said, Tomatis tore out a blank page, placed it on the table under the light of the lamp, cleaned the point of his pen, tested it out on the margin of his geometry notebook and then, slowly, with great care, feeling Barco's gaze over his shoulder fixed on his steady hand holding the pen, he wrote in great black printed letters the word: MESSAGE; and, as his hand continued moving from right to left, the blank rectangular page passed from extreme whiteness, undifferentiated, from limbo, from a flat and anonymous horizon, selected by chance by a blind hand from among a mountain of identical sheets that lay dusty and mute in the desk drawer, until the word was written, neat and even, and the identity of the page was erased once again, consumed by the intermediate darkness of the message.

The next day they woke at dawn. Tomatis phoned Barco to tell him that in a minute he was headed down to catch the streetcar, that Barco should wait for the next number two car because that was the one he was taking, and soon he saw Barco, through the streetcar window, on the corner, carrying a shovel, the bottle, and a bar of sealing wax. For his part, Tomatis had brought a can of sardines, some tomatoes and peaches, and a bottle of wine he had taken from the fridge. He carried the message, folded into quarters, carefully in the right-hand pocket of his shirt. They arrived at the club, donned their bathing suits, put everything but the shovel in a canvas bag, put the bag and the shovel at the bottom of a canoe, and then pushed the canoe into the river. Barco began rowing, pushing away from the club dock and the suspension bridge and setting a course between the islets and tributaries, skirting the shore that frequently closed in around them, and when at last he was directing the boat with some degree of mastery and had begun to approach the coast it was already past eleven. Barco's face was red, his body covered in sweat. The sun was white, arid, and its rays perforated the naturally porous and open canopy of weeping willows, projecting patches of light onto the water. They left the canoe in the shade—it caught the patches of light on its bottom—and made their way inland with the shovel and the canvas bag. They wandered for half an hour. Barco discovered a snake and with the edge of the shovel he completely severed its head, neatly, in a single blow; afterward they chose the spot. It was a clearing surrounded by a circle of trees, but trees so short that their branches couldn't tangle together to form a shaded bower. The sun had dried the ground and the grass around was sparse and yellowed. Tomatis began to dig: the first few impacts sounded dry and the shovel bounced back from the ground, breaking its shell and sending up chips of hardened clay in every direction, but the outer layer gave way quickly and then the earth came deep, soft, cold, and dark, its weight pulling Tomatis's arms softly downward every time he hoisted a shovelful and dumped it onto the mound that had begun to form to the side of the hole. After a while Barco took over and Tomatis leaned panting against one of the absurd trees and dedicated himself to watching him work. They dug a hole almost six feet deep, wide enough for a man to enter standing. Afterward they sat in the shade and Barco carefully folded the sheet of paper, pushed it down the neck of the bottle, replaced the cork, slapping it with the palm of his hand until he got it in far enough, and in a moment readied the sealing wax and the matches, and lighting one, began spinning the bar of wax on the point of the flame, taking care that the drops of wax fell directly onto the bottle's spout and the rounded top of the cork. They used up a lot of matches before it was done. Tomatis's gaze fell alternately on the point of flame melting the wax (sometimes it followed the path of the red wax drops that glittered as they splattered over the spout of the bottle, droplets that Barco ended up filling in and spreading out with the softened end of the bar) and on the interior of the bottle, in which was still visible, through the green glass, the sheet of paper folded so many times it looked like a rigid strip of tape, one end standing on the base of the bottle and the other on the green wall, at a diagonal. Even when Barco moved the bottle, the paper stayed where it was. And when he finished, Barco picked it up and held it with such delicacy that Tomatis wondered if Barco wasn't just clowning around again, but then, seeing him move toward the hole carrying the bottle in both hands, and afterward kneel next to the mouth of the hole and lean in, inserting the hand that held the bottle in order to deposit it as smoothly as possible at the bottom, almost touching his forehead to the ground, Tomatis understood that Barco wasn't joking, and if perhaps he wasn't going as far as solemnity, he was at least disposed to smoothly and simply follow things through. Barco dropped the bottle on the bottom, considered the result of the fall, judged it adequate, and then stood up and began to pour dirt back into the hole with the shovel. After a time he passed the shovel to Tomatis, and when the hole was full to the brim, he took the shovel in his hands again and began to smooth down the top, trying to erase the evidence of their excavation.

"If it rains tonight," He said when he finished, leaning on the shovel and mopping his sweat, "by tomorrow there won't be a trace left on the ground."

And it did rain. Tomatis heard it drumming against the roof as he lay in the dark of his room on the landing. When they finished they had put the shovel back in the bottom of the canoe and then gone for a swim, eaten the sardines and the peaches and drunk the bottle of wine, slept a while beneath the trees and then returned, rowing slowly, taking turns, the river below, arriving so late that when they moored the canoe at the club dock, surrounded by a cloud of mosquitoes, it was already dusk, blue and full of noises and voices coming from the beach and the lit-up bar. They took the streetcar home and Barco jumped off and disappeared through the door of his house. Tomatis took a cold shower, ate something, and went to bed. Almost instantly he fell asleep. More than the sound, it was the smell of the rain that woke him, making the heated roof tiles crackle, and afterward the freshness, the fullness of the water coming in through the open window. As he became more lucid, Tomatis thought of the bottle buried in the darkness of the earth, just as he himself was buried in the darkness of the world, and he asked himself what the fate of the bottle would be. Because it could happen that whoever found it might speak some other language, or the same language in which, nevertheless, the word "message" would have a different meaning, even the opposite meaning from what they had intended, even the meaning of "information" that Barco had wanted to eliminate, or possibly that no one would find the bottle at all, the race of men would be blotted from the earth, and the bottle would remain forever buried inside a dry, empty planet, spinning in the darkness of space. But finally, just before falling asleep, Tomatis considered that even when men capable of understanding it might encounter their message, it would not contain them, Barco and Tomatis, just as it would not contain the crashing waves, in the slow smacks of the canoe at each firm stroke of the oar, the lit-up bar they made out from the dock engulfed in blue darkness, and the scent of fresh rain that came in through the window, in gusts, at that very moment.

Letter to the Seer

In the grand tradition of the enlightened, I occupy, always, the last place. I'm not speaking in a chronological sense, but hierarchically: sleepiness, drowsiness, myopia fill my resumé. From Petronio's frenetic maelstrom I have retained no more than a sentence: "A day is nothing: there is just time to become yourself, and then night is upon you." In those conditions laziness is not so much a vice as an ontological subject. So then, what does a man see between two dreams, when he has not yet freed himself of the first to fall immediately into the second? He sees nothing. Because seeing, madam, is not a matter of contemplating, inert, the tireless passage of apparitions, but of seizing, from those apparitions, some meaning. In a word, the vertical work, like that of the ray, of the enlightened one, which you know and employ, or, really, that which employs you. For that reason I came to you saying that in the grand tradition of the enlightened, I, always, invisible, occupy the last place.

Sleepiness, drowsiness, myopia: and the hand, too, that, in this semidarkness, moves, errs, closing, opening, showing openly, easily, how it has grasped nothing. The greatness, the subspecies, related to sleepiness and the hand, is, you will have already guessed, darkness. The great black magnetic mass that drags our gestures downward, one by one. In that blackness, the world, I accomplish my designated task, clumsily, according to the rules. My muse, if I may call her that, is, if you like, a manual. The subtle mechanics of the ray, if, from time to time, it touches me, are useless among so much darkness.

So I send you nothing. Nothing to submit to your clairvoyance. The monotonous, dull universe has nothing to do with the monotonous, dull fragments in me. And if I speak now, this once, unmediated, in the first person, it is in order to demonstrate clearly that through me no otherness shall be manifest, nothing that is not in the fleeting stains; fugitive, intermittent, whose borders are invaded by darkness, and which we call the world. From this purblind letter, I ask you to draw no conclusion. Because a conclusion is always behind and is, in relation to its parts, an "other." Now then, for a blind man there can certainly be otherness, unity, everything. A blind man enjoys his right to imagination. A myopic man should be modest: a mobile stain occupies the entirety of his reduced field of vision and annihilates, without malignancy, everything else. The blind man, as far as he is from the world, can, with a vertiginous imagination, grasp it. The myopic man is too close to the remaining fragments to escape, in a leap, his plain.

What can be expected, then, from a dozing man? Nothing more than a series of fragments, dense, uncut. Let the world shine in them, if one of the ways of the world is to shine.

Half-Erased

For Bernard le Gonidec

A harsh diagonal column of light comes in through the window and settles, on the wood floor, in a yellow circle inside of which a million pale particles wheel around, while the smoke of my cigarette, rising from the bed, enters it and slowly disperses, on this May morning, from which I can see, through the window, the blue sky: insomnia. I'll get up in a while, take the clothes off of my brother's empty bed, get dressed, go out into the street for my first cup of coffee at the galleria, smoking my third or fourth cigarette of the day, standing next to the counter, looking down the way, not speaking, not tasting either the coffee or the smoke, a man about thirty years old to those who see me from the outside, sometimes mistaken for my brother—someone will surely come along to greet me thinking I am him and not me, the one I know myself to be— and through the windows of the galleria I will see the sunlight falling onto the red metal tables in the practically empty patio: the workday. I contemplate—having overcome my bewilderment at being alive, still, and awake, again—the room being divided in two by this diagonal column of light, and I see the furniture, my own clothes, my brother's empty bed, the light itself, the smoke: separation. At once, suddenly, rapidly, resonating even more intensely than my own silence and louder than my silence can bear, from what my mother calls the foyer, the phone rings. From afar, Héctor's voice asks if I heard the explosions last night, and I use my voice for the first time today to say that the first explosion went off as Tomatis and I were standing in the doorway of the game room at the Progress club, and that when the second one went off we were playing *truco* and the cards on the table, on the green felt, were the ace against the king on top, and the jack against the knight below. Life imitates art, Héctor says, adding that he'll come pick me up in half an hour to go see where the dynamite has opened breaches along the coast road. Standing on the sidewalk I see the car approaching in the sun, the cigarette between my lips and the smoke dissipating just above my face—standing on the piece of sidewalk that I have just been contemplating from the balcony, having hung up the phone and gotten dressed—into the air, sunny and windless, but cold. The car moves ahead among others like it, black, slow, and its chrome sparkles in the sun. It is just another particle of the monotonous noise generated, for some time, by the city, a particle of the tumult of staining and shifting that has begun to work early this morning. We go straight, slowly, stopping every minute among the cars that follow us and those that cross in front of us, and when we get to the central post office and the bus station, we turn onto the Avenida del Puerto and start speeding up, freeing ourselves from the cramped nucleus of the city, seeing the palm trees come toward us and then fall behind, grayed and fraying at the onset of winter. The car's side windows are foggy. The hard light of the sun breaks at sharp right angles upon the trees and houses. The men walking along the sidewalks and others, working on the beach as longshoremen, are bathed, so to speak, in the cold light. Leaning forward, Héctor has taken out, from the glove compartment, a flask of cognac, offering me a sip. I have refused it. Still, he has given me the flask, covered in hard leather, so that, as he drives, I can unscrew the metal cap. The smell of alcohol floods my nose, even colder than the air I was just breathing on the sidewalk and that still scratches my nostrils. Beyond Héctor's profile, raised in the act of drinking, even beyond the foggy glass, there is a white wall passing, recently painted, endless, and behind it I know there are men, at this very moment, making blocks of ice. The rough pavement makes the white image tremble in the dingy window. And suddenly, calmly, I remember a dream, as if someone had offered me a glimpse inside a barely open box, only to slam it shut just as I leaned in, just as I've begun to guess what's inside. I don't remember what the dream was about, just that I have had it. It seems to me that there was no white wall in it, no car, nor was Héctor in the dream, nor, moreover, did it take place on the Avenida del Puerto, and yet I remembered it, for a moment, when I looked, beyond the raised profile and beyond the dingy window, at the white wall. A policeman, cloaked and serious, refuses, at the suspension bridge, to let us pass. It seems it is uncertain whether or not the water, flooding up over the breaches, will block the road. Héctor takes a press pass from the glove compartment and hands it to the policeman, whose face, the color of wood, half hidden between the rim of his cap and the collar of his coat, peers through the window. At last we cross the bridge, heading onto the road, surrounded on either side, as far as the eye can see, by water: water, and sometimes, in the middle of a field, a farmhouse in ruins, of which we can just make out the roof and a bit of the walls; not even the tops of the trees; everything else is water, smooth and calm, level with the embankment. When we get to the first breach we stop the car and get out. The noise of the car doors opening, the sound of our voices and our shoes scraping against the asphalt strewn with rubble rings out and then fades. Héctor talks about science fiction. Then, as we are bent over the rubble watching the torrent flow—in what direction?—through the breach, where the two liquid plains join, almost soundlessly, he recalls Faulkner. Too much literature for a painter, I say. Héctor doesn't answer me. He removes the flask from his bag and takes another sip of cognac, wrinkling his elastic face. I draw my dull gaze from the torrent at the depths of the breach to the two smooth expanses divided by the road. They tell me nothing. For the first few days I tried to feel bewilderment, even fear, pity for those who the water would sweep away, something, but I managed nothing. I see nothing but a smooth surface, almost placid, extending to the horizon from each edge of the road strewn with rubble, and it gives me no sign. The thing that really makes me shudder, says Héctor, is to think this idea we have that the water must, at some point, stop rising and begin to recede might be utterly wrong. In the middle of the street, the black car, its chrome sparkling in the sun, its doors open, looks as if it had been abandoned long ago. It looks, so to speak, dead. And we, the only moving things in this harsh, monotonous landscape, have also fallen still. A helicopter appears. It wheels over our heads a couple times before heading back toward the city, fading from view. The pilot must have seen us from above, two men dressed in black overcoats, in full sunlight, squatting amid the rubble, looking at the breach in the embankment, and the black car abandoned in the middle of the road, its chrome resplendent in the sun, its doors open. We turn around slowly, cautiously avoiding the water, and once we are pointed in the opposite direction we start heading back to the city. As we leave the bridge behind us and Héctor gives a friendly wave to the policeman who intercepted us on our way out, I see the helicopter passing over our heads again and heading toward the other side of the bridge, flying over the road in the direction of the breaches in the embankment. The delicate frame, red metal and glass, flies low, and I wonder what the pilot must see from above, apart from the breaches and the rubble and the blue strip of asphalt and the two liquid plains. All of that without us, without the black car, I mean, and then, as we begin to drive back along the Avenida del Puerto, Héctor tells me not to worry, that while the water continues to rise—and the radio bulletin, at precisely that moment, says that it is still rising, and will continue to rise—I can stay perfectly calm because, after all, in four days I will be in Paris. I know that he's watching me intently, with no regard for the road, to see what effect his words have had on me—or at least I assume that if he is watching me so intently, it is for that reason—but I keep staring at the white wall through the dingy window. Really, his words have had no effect on me. I feel as if the tips of everything metal were rippling, now that the sun is almost at its zenith. I haven't had coffee. Héctor suggests we have lunch together. During the meal, Héctor says, I think, that travel will do me good, take me out of myself a bit. Then he starts, out of habit, to talk about Cat. I think Cat, he says, just doesn't want to grow up. Predictable end for Cat: a nuthouse. He asks me if I will see him before I leave. And as Héctor talks at the other end of the table, from above his head and his elastic face, above his perfectly cleaned and coiffed hair, the tumult of the restaurant, of which we, too, form a part, the homogeneous noise of the interior where we sit is like an orchestral accompaniment, a base that improves Héctor's voice, it seems to me, slightly. There is a deafening cacophony of noise. Someone in a gray overcoat, clean-shaven, opens the front door and enters, followed by two women. He approaches our table, removing his black leather gloves. I feel his cold hand when I shake it, because Héctor has introduced him to me. He's a painter from Buenos Aires or something like that; he has the air of someone who is moving up in the world, or has moved up in the world, economically speaking. The two women linger by the door, taking off their coats. They talk about something they were doing together last night at the time of the explosions. They have been, it seems, at a party or something like that. They mention something that happened, something funny, it seems, because they laugh and Héctor, who is standing next to his chair—just like me, leaning over, with my knees half bent, my left hand holding a glass of wine—says that when I heard the first explosion I was entering the games room at the Progress Club with Tomatis, and that, according to me, when the second explosion went off, the cards on the table were the ace winning against the king on top, the jack and the knight below. And I told him, says Héctor. I told him: Art imitates life. The man throws his head back when he laughs, exposing his shaved neck. Then he leaves. He sits with the women at a table behind Héctor's head, and I continue to see them the whole time beyond his elastic face, while Héctor is talks about Cat. Not just growing up: Cat has never shown a real or consistent interest in any serious pursuit his whole life. He's too mercurial. Héctor keeps talking, but all the while food is disappearing from his plate. At last he uses a piece of bread to soak up the red sauce, leaving the white porcelain streaked with red lines, dry and flecked with white. The food must be gathering now in his stomach, which has begun to work in its own way. Two or three discrete belches attest to this work. Then Héctor adjusts his chair and lights, having meticulously prepared it beforehand, a pipe. I smoke a cigarette. Héctor seems to be reflecting on the things he has just said about Cat, as if it is the first time he has said them and he is trying to polish them, mull them over in his mind to reformulate them more precisely. But he has already formed them many times, with that same disjointed style, with that same rhetoric doubly weakened by lack of conviction and repetition. Something about the imminent winter settling down outside has invaded the restaurant, and I think for a moment, fragmentarily, about the breaches in the embankment, opened onto the coastal road, about the asphalt, cracked at the borders and strewn with rubble all around. I think that Héctor must not have looked at me this whole time. I think that he has not even looked at the smoke from his pipe as it unwinds slowly before his face, a blue smoke, and that what he seems to be contemplating now, with his half-closed eyes, is neither the blue smoke nor any present point, nor my face. So entering the games room at the Progress Club with

Tomatis, he says, brusquely. Yes, I say. His elastic face flinches from the smoke, and it is obvious how the skin there has worn away and wrinkled over the years. More than feeling unfamiliar, I tell him, then, when he asks me how I will feel abroad, I will have to deal with the unfamiliar thought that a city where I was born and where I have lived nearly thirty years will continue living without me, and then I say that a city is an abstraction we concede to so we can give a particular name to a series of places that are fragmentary, unconnected, lifeless, and that most often exist in imaginary time, bereft of us. And then, slowly at first, timid, polished and perfected through continuous repetition, like the foot of a marble saint smoothed by the kisses of interminable pilgrims, in an order that varies less and less, the stream of Héctor's memories of Europe: his three years living in Paris, first on the rue des Ciseaux, then on the rue Gassendi, his summers in Italy, his expositions in London, in Amsterdam, in Copenhagen. One of them was attended by Matta, the Chilean surrealist, whom he connected with Breton. He had been to Breton's house several times, had translated surrealist texts that Edgar Bayley tried to have published in a magazine that recently went out of business. As we leave the restaurant, this stream continues monotonously. In the street, as we walk toward the car, on the sidewalk in front of the Municipal theater, wide and warmed by the sun, another of our friends stops us, extending an icy hand: have we heard the noon bulletin saying that the water is still rising, and will continue to rise? We respond that we had heard the explosions; we've also heard the bulletin. Shaking his cold hand again. In the car, having started the motor, we take turns sipping from the leather-covered flask until we've emptied it, putting it back into the glove compartment. Héctor doesn't talk anymore. He holds the pipe, unlit, between his teeth, like a rigid, slightly more polished appendage, the same color as the inhuman material of his face. I've just put out my cigarette, and there is a strong, diffused scent of ash in the car. With the motor on, the heater gets going. There is a clear contrast between the cold light outside and the hot, contaminated air inside the car. Now we have reached the southern tip of the city, Boca del Tigre. There is a checkpoint at the convergence of three avenues, and behind the checkpoint the bridge and the highway. On either side of the bridge, water. Closer, to our left, in the huge open space before the soccer stadium, tents, an encampment, military vehicles, an interminable disorder of objects: beds, dressers, paintings, chairs, pots, carts, quilts, animals, people. The sun warms this dismantled anthill. Héctor talks about Marché aux puces and Hôtel Drouot, Parisian markets for secondhand goods, highly surrealist places. He quotes Discépolo from *Tango Cambalache*: you'll see the Bible weeping against a water heater.[1] It follows that reality itself is surrealistic, though he has renounced surrealism because too great a love for objects disrupts metaphysical reflection. But the genius of objects, he says, they have it. They have it. Objects tend to gel together, they are gregarious, he says. Adornments are to objects as nineteenth century realism is to surrealism. Still, he, Héctor, he says, is looking for a new way, a third position. Thus, when he is interviewed, he says, laughing, when asked what school of art he belongs to, he responds: Justicialism. When he drops me off at my door, he tells me he will be at his studio at 8 p.m. sharp. I am passing through the little room my mother calls the anteroom when the phone rings. Elisa's voice asks me if Cat has come back from El Rincón. I tell her that he hasn't. She asks me if the explosions went off in El Rincón, and I tell her, no, they were much closer to the city, two or three kilometers from the suspension bridge, long before you get to La Guardia, and that I've just come back from seeing the resulting breaches with Héctor, before lunch. Elisa asks

1. *Tango Cambalache* (Junkshop Tango), 1935

if Héctor is with me and I tell her that we just parted, that I don't
know where he's gone. With my husband, you never know, Elisa
says, although you can very well imagine. I'm not sure what to say,
so I say nothing. After a short, mutually reproving silence, we say
our goodbyes and hang up. I smoke for around an hour in bed,
thinking. My overcoat and my jacket lie on Cat's empty bed. The
room is filled with smoke. Through the spotless windows, I see the
cold light recede. From the other side of the house drifts the sound
of television. It is a dull mix of voices and music. From the street,
on the other hand, the homogenous murmur, familiar, identical to,
although perhaps more profound than this morning, and which
will tear itself apart in the evening, rises and resounds. I listen to it
for a moment, I focus my attention on it, but it doesn't leave the
slightest impression. Against the wall, on the other side of the bed,
is my suitcase, packed since yesterday, next to the blue coat. I have
shut it under the impatient gaze of Tomatis, who, I think, was playing with his gloves, bringing them with his fingers up to his face
and then letting them fall upon his knees. Or perhaps not, perhaps
he was smacking his knees with them, or the palm of his hand. It
was probably the palm of his hand, or perhaps his chest. Or even
his face, because he was lying face up on Cat's bed while I packed
the suitcase, impatient to go out to eat, or more precisely to go out,
because later, as we were eating, he was also impatient and wanted
to go I-don't-even-know-where. Some place other than where we
were, I suppose, some place where he, I mean, was not at that
moment, thinking perhaps that he should walk around for a few
minutes to get under control—I'm not sure if I'm being clear here—
because it preoccupied him to know that wherever he was, there
was a mountain of other places he wasn't at all. I get up and put the
ashtray, which had been balancing on my chest, on the nightstand.
In this room there is a bluish semi-darkness. I must have been lying
here almost an hour. I walk around the room a bit and then poke

my head out the window: on the sidewalk before me murky figures are passing in front of a shop window with six television sets, all identical, all on. On all six, arranged in two rows of three, one on top of the other, the same flickering image appears, steel blue, the enormous head of a man crying, his face buried in his hands. I recognize the afternoon soap opera. Then I step back from the window, cross through the blue bedroom and the little room my mother calls the foyer, through the living room, where, for a moment, I interrupt my mother's field of vision as she watches the man crying. When I get to the study, I turn on the light. There are two empty desks, one facing each window, so that when Cat and I would sit down to work, we would be back to back. From Cat's window one can see the brick-colored tile terraces, patios with dark trees, the white municipal building against the red splendor of the sky. Mine looks out onto an interior patio with yellow and blue tiles lined up against the wall. I'm standing under the light hanging from the ceiling, between two windows, in front of the bookshelf. I'm not looking at anything in particular. Now that I am sitting before my desk and, opening the top drawer, I take out a few blank sheets. At the desk I lift up a green ballpoint pen and write: Dear Cat. I was going to pass by El Rincón to see you but I didn't have time. I can only hope you aren't up to your neck in water. It looks like you will be soon enough. I hope you've got some news from Washington. Mama won't be too much work while I'm gone: wake her up after the end of the daily broadcast on TV and tell her she can go to bed now, and turn down the volume for her every once in a while during viewing hours. As always, I am well, and I'll write to you as soon as I get settled in Paris. Tonight they're throwing me a goodbye party at Héctor's studio (he told me not to tell you about it) and I guess I have to stop here because I'm going to be late. A hug. Pigeon. Now I open the drawer to Cat's desk to leave the note and I see the photograph: there we are, in t-shirts, smiling at the camera, six or seven years old, Cat or me, because I can't tell anymore which of the two appears there, with part of the house in El Rincón, white, behind us, to the left, and to the right, further off, a few willows and the river. You have to be inside to know which one you are, and in this photo, Cat or me, it must be twenty years ago, in a T-shirt, laughing at the camera, is outside. There is another photo, identical, not a copy but another photo, or perhaps a copy, in one of my desk drawers. Some distant relative took them both, the same day, in the same pose, in the same place, a few minutes apart, not having foresight like my mother, who wasted her youth planting clues all over the world that would help distinguish us; he sent the pictures to us a few months later. As I am passing again through the living room, intercepting the television screen with my body, my mother tells me, according to the bulletin in the afternoon, that the military has exploded dynamite along the coast road to allow the water to flow out and reduce the pressure that has been building for days against the suspension bridge, threatening to sweep it away. She asks me if I have heard the explosions. Now I am putting on my jacket, slowly, and then my overcoat. I close the door behind me, putting on my gloves. It's utterly dark outside. The murmur fades. Standing in front of the counter of the bar in the galleria, I drink a cognac, slowly, smoking. There's hardly anybody here. The cashier, dressed in green overalls, flips through a comic book. A man eats green olives from a plate and drinks vermouth, sitting at one of the tables in the hall. Now that I am in the taxi headed toward Héctor's studio, it occurs to me that I am no longer in the room with the two desks, the room with the two beds, or intercepting the screen with my body as I pass through the living room, or standing in the bar in the galleria. Nor am I in the place where I began thinking, because the taxi is cutting through the cold night and leaves behind street corners fading ever darker. Yet, having stood for a moment between the two desks, under the light, or crossing the living room, intercepting the blue steel of the television screen with my body, I am struck by the fact that the living room and the room with the desks are still in their places, emptied of me, at this very moment. Of all the things in this world, I am the least real. Moving an inch, I am erased. And I see, as we move away from the city, through the streets growing darker and darker, more and more deserted, through the frosty glass, the fixed neighborhoods on whose sidewalks leafless trees expose their ruins to the first frost. Constant and practically lifeless, soundless, a straggling light from a pharmacy or a corner store that shines on the sidewalk, a quick message shouted from one side of the street to the other, a car passing on a cross street, they extend around me, as I pass through rapidly, these neighborhoods that persist. Héctor comes forward to receive me when I clap my hands to announce I've arrived. There's still no one around. He has invited the whole world, he tells me, to come at nine. He says that he wanted to set up the grill and talk to me in peace. All of the lights in the studio are lit and the white, arid walls refract the light and compound its clarity. Only the very top lies in darkness. On the back patio, while he watches over the fire and the meat, and the smoke pries tears from his eyes that dry into the folds of his elastic face, Héctor, who has laid a bottle of wine and two glasses on top of a table covered in a white piece of paper, says that if the water continues to rise, the highway from Boca del Tigre will be cut off and the bus taking me to Buenos Aires won't be able to get through. I tell him not to exaggerate and Héctor laughs. He's a bit drunk; weepy. He says that exaggeration is an art form. Cat has perfected it, he says. He does everything too well, he says, Cat does, and he is too well provided for to be capable, even when he tries, and he has tried, moreover, many times, to stick with something. We return to the shed and Héctor shows me the painting he is finishing. It is an arid, white rectangle that in no way differs from the white walls of the studio.

It is perhaps a bit whiter and more arid than the walls. The white-ness of the walls has, on the one hand, it seems to me, the purpose of suggesting a certain width, as well as a certain height; in the painting, the horizontal quality is, I have the impression, so to speak, erased. Its whiteness is exclusively vertical. I don't know if I have seen this or if it was Héctor himself who told me so this morn-ing. In Héctor's paintings, everything is vertical; not ascending, not descending, just vertical. Serving glasses of wine in the open air by the fire in the back patio, Héctor smokes his pipe and tries to explain to me what it is he wanted to express. We are interrupted by someone clapping their hands in the entrance. It is Raquel. She kisses us quickly on the cheek and disappears into the studio. She returns without her coat and with an empty wineglass in her hand. After taking her first sip of wine she asks us, looking more at Héc-tor, if we heard the explosions last night. Héctor responds that he was with people, at a party, and that I, when the first explosion went off, was with Tomatis, passing through the door to the games room at the Progress Club. He says that when the second went off the cards on the table were the ace and the king on top, the jack and the knight below, Héctor says. And I told him that life imitates art, he says. For a moment, while the meat crackles over the coals and the smoke rises in a dense, diagonal column, we smoke in silence, taking small sips of wine. Raquel asks me how I feel now that I'm about to leave for Paris. I say nothing. Raquel's green wool dress hugs her thick body. We are, so to speak, almost cold, between total exposure and the hot splendor of the coals. Héctor starts up again about Cat. Cat is the plague, says Raquel, laughing. A new interruption: Héctor disappears toward the front door, and there comes an increasingly loud tumult of familiar voices, male and female. Quiet, we look at the fire. Now, before Héctor and the recent arrivals appear on the patio, other knocks at the door ring out and the voices multiply. They are all too familiar for us to pay attention to them. In a low voice, Raquel asks me if we could get a drink alone together after the party. Before I can answer, Héctor reappears on the patio. He invites us to come inside. The recent arrivals, six all together, contemplate, arranged in a semicircle before the easel, Héctor's latest painting, the white surface. They admire it, each in his or her own way. Now the semicircle breaks apart and we greet each other in scattered groups. We talk about the explosions. The night bulletin, someone says, has reported that the water is still rising, and will continue to rise. Alicia, dressed in blue, disappears toward the patio, because Héctor has been called away for a moment to the door. He watches us serenely, his pipe in his mouth, jutting out from his elastic face. At the very moment Alicia disappears, Elisa comes through the front door, without knocking. She greets us seriously, but not coldly. Kissing me on the cheek, I feel her tense a little, as if she were saving for me the little hostility of which she is capable, or perhaps because she has seen, over my shoulder, just as she kissed me, Alicia appear on the patio, followed by Héctor's misty eyes, which contrast against his dried up, elastic face. At the table, Elisa sits to my right, Raquel across from me. Like a spontaneous, stable, even warm radiation, Elisa's hostility crashes constantly against my circumspect profile, which sometimes turns, gently, toward her, and rebounds against her wide, stony face. No one who doesn't know us well, who isn't habituated to our most intimate particularities, and sometimes even under those conditions, is able to tell us apart, Cat and I, and even we ourselves look at photographs in our desk drawers and doubt the mirror in which we contemplate ourselves reciprocally, identical, and she, who for at least five years has been thinking day and night about Cat, who has been sleeping with him two or three times a week for at least two years, cannot be less than two meters from me without starting to radiate repugnance and hostility. It's as if I were the inverse of Cat. And he will stay: he will keep waking up every morning beside the river, in the house in El Rincón, will pass through the bars of the city getting drunk until morning, and he will pass through the door of the games room at the Progress Club with Tomatis, he will look at the white municipal building sitting at his desk, not reading or writing anything, and then he will go out onto the street to meet her, to stretch himself out over her, naked, in some hotel, in the house in El Rincón, where Héctor knows he shouldn't go without calling first, as do I, greeting, on the corner of San Martín and Mendoza, someone who has wished him a good afternoon thinking he is me, he will be standing on the corner in the afternoon, in a T-shirt, freshly bathed, in the summer, smoking. Héctor talks about the breaches. He has seen them, he says, with me, this morning. They are several meters wide and the crumbling borders look like the mouth of a volcano; all the asphalt is strewn with rubble; they are inspecting the area with helicopters, and all around, up to the horizon, smooth, monotonous, yellowing, rising ever higher, is the water. Someone tells us that he was sleeping at the moment the first explosion went off; another, making love. One of them asks me where I was when I heard them; I was with Tomatis in the games room of the Progress Club, I say. Now some people walk across the great white shed that, apart from the easel with the painting, the disordered tables and chairs, contains practically nothing. I am sitting on a divan jutting out from the wall, between Raquel and Alicia. I see people, from afar, who cross the shed, groups that converse, laughing faces coming toward me, and talking to me: from time to time when I serve myself wine and smoke, I talk. The words form between my teeth and my lips, so that they slip out half chewed, half smoked. Even so, at this time, I am not absent; I am here. Nowhere else. Here. I see Elisa go out; she has said goodbye to some people, not to everyone, not to me. It must have been to avoid coming close to Alicia. I see her dress, red and blue flowers printed on a white background, disappear beneath her overcoat, and then the rest of her disappears, suddenly, through the front door. Now the huge white shed is practically deserted. Héctor, Alicia, and a couple are standing in front of the easel, looking at the arid, white, vertical rectangle. Slowly, at a diagonal, someone crosses the empty shed, and goes to sit in a chair, behind the easel. Raquel is stretched out on the divan, her head in my lap, her eyes closed; her hand, hanging over the side of the divan, holds a cigarette that burns out on its own, sending up smoke between her fingers. The four figures, standing out starkly against the broad background, speak in low voices and sometimes shake their heads or lift a hand, that they immediately drop, indicating, without enthusiasm, the painting. Now there are no more than four of us in the studio. Héctor, Alicia, Raquel and I, looking, without speaking, for a moment, in the same direction, at the white wall before us, from the other side of the empty shed where the brick floor ends. Now the light goes out. I see the form of Raquel's body stretched out beside mine, in the reddish semidarkness produced by the electric stove by the divan. The white walls, in the semidarkness, emit a weak phosphorescence. The white painting, from far away, is, so to speak, like a window from which one is watching the sunrise. I feel, from beneath her dress, Raquel's warm, slightly loose flesh. Now we are naked, covered by a blanket. From the attic noises filter down to us of the wood of the floor and the bed creaking, hushed voices, laughter, and later cries and moans from Alicia. Hearing them, Raquel lets out a short cry, which she muffles by pressing her mouth against my shoulder. It remains there for a moment. There is a mouth against my shoulder, open, the same mouth that hours before has asked me to go with her to get a drink after the party. The mouth descends my right arm to my elbow and stops there. Her whole body has been fidgeting beneath the blanket. Now that the mouth has paused on my arm, she is quiet. Nothing comes from the attic. Her body, standing, bending, moves a little, before her mouth begins to move, now that the mouth moves from my arm to my belly and even a little lower. The mouth begins to make some noises that resound in the empty shed. I catch a glimpse of Cat sleeping in El Rincón. He is not me, so that I am not him either, he who is standing on the corner, in summer, in a T-shirt, freshly bathed, nodding to someone who has confused him for me. A summer so large that, so to speak, I cannot fill it completely. The mouth, without a body, without me, works, with a regular rhythm, in the reddish semidarkness, while my confused thoughts intermix, the way an insomniac experiences a vivid dream and then, slowly, begins to wake. The light is on again now, Raquel and I beneath the blanket, naked, and Héctor and Alicia, dressed, standing beside the stove, facing the divan. We make space at the end of the table, among the remains of the cold food, and we sit down to snack, sipping wine. Raquel's mouth receives the pieces of cold meat, chews them slowly, flashes her tongue when she licks her wrinkled lips, talks. Héctor speaks, once in Paris, they, too, had held a barbeque in an *atelier* that he shared with a Greek painter, a surrealist. The painter was a lesbian. She smoked cigarettes. She drank kirsch and, at dawn, went out onto the street to steal the milk bottles deliverymen left on the doorsteps of groceries. Now he turns to me: is it true, that story Cat would tell about the brother of our great-grandfather who was an intern in a hospital in Buenos Aires during the yellow fever outbreak, and who, according to Cat, abandoned his post for fear of the contagion and appeared in the city, in our great-great-grandfather's house, no one knowing what in the world he was doing there; and who, according to Cat, says Héctor, had brought the fever with him and died four days later, spreading the plague? Héctor asks me if it is true. I say that if Cat said it, it must be true. Héctor laughs. They are quite different, says Alicia. Cat is the plague, says Raquel. That glut, that abandon, that oblivion, that death, is necessary so that one may begin, gradually, like a sun, to rise up, tracing a parabola with a zenith and a nadir, with its own rhythm, at the time when histories are intertwined, confused, superimposed, corrected, perfected, falsified, in a cold dawn in an illuminated shed with white walls, heated by electric stoves. Cat, who, once, at the School of Fine Arts, shattered a cast of the Venus de Milo; the time Cat and I shared the same woman, and we alternated weeks sleeping with her, convincing her that we were the same person; the version Cat came up with, in which the woman also had a twin sister, who switched off with her to receive us; the man who, last year, threw himself out the window of the courthouse after being sentenced by the judge, my cousin; the time during which Héctor and the lesbian made copies of famous paintings and sold them on the Pont des Arts; stories about Washington. Fixed, closed, we shuffle them like cards for two hours. They move from mouth to mouth, like passwords. They have been, so to speak, polished so much, like stones, their contours so precise, distinguished so easily from one another, that it is as if, at a certain moment, they stop being stories, things that have happened in space and time, and turn into objects, algae, blossoms. It is easy, since they are already in the past. But what is happening in time, what is happening now, the time of the stories we remain inside, is inexpressible. Now we are standing again before the arid, vertical rectangle. Héctor, whose elastic face has grayed a bit, traces imaginary vertical lines before the canvas with the mouthpiece of his pipe. Raquel asks if it took him a long time to paint it. A month of Sundays, says Héctor. Now we are sitting again at the corner of the table, drinking coffee. Héctor drops a lump of sugar into a glass of water and we sit watching it dissolve. The objective *durée*, says Héctor. The what? asks Alicia. The objective *durée*. The *durée*. *Durée*. Duration, says Héctor. To be objective, says Héctor, one must measure it, one must be present. His painting, he says, is an amplified fragment of the objective *durée*. At the bottom of the glass there remains a sandy sediment of little crystals. Then nothing more. The glass alone remains, with the water, without any *durée*. Look: not even a trace of the objective *durée*, says Héctor. To listen to Héctor, who has explained the meaning of the painting, I have reverted my gaze to his elastic face, taking it from the glass. When I look back at it, there is at first the sandy sediment and then nothing: the glass with the water, with no *durée*. Now Raquel and I are heading out into the icy dawn, toward Raquel's car, parked on the other side of the deserted avenue. The interior of the car is freezing. As the motor warms up, Raquel lights a cigarette and passes it to me, and then lights another that she leaves hanging in her mouth. Now we have pulled up in front of my house. You'll laugh at me, she says. You'll tell me not be pushy, but this is stronger than me. You'll be wanting kids one of these days, sometime, with someone, I say. She says she'll be at the station the day after tomorrow, at ten to twelve, to see me off. And now that I am lying down, smoking, through the window I see the cold blue sky, a ray of sun, full of a million dancing particles, passing through the glass to draw a clear circle on the parquet. My clothes lie on Cat's untouched bed. Standing next to the desk, I see, through the window, the white apartment block, vertical and full of dark rectangular perforations, the municipal building. Now I'm looking at the ferns on the patio, the flowerpots lined up along the yellow walls. There is light in the patio, but not a single patch of sun. I am standing next to the counter at the bar, in the galleria, looking at the cashier dressed in green overalls. The owner of the bar comes out of the back room with an empty glass in his hand, which he puts down on the coffee machine. At the bottom my cup still holds a trace of coffee. The owner of the bar says something to me, in a vague way, which is typical of him, I think because he is never sure whether he is talking to me or to Cat. He talks about the explosions, doubting the results: they should have waited, he says, until the water got to the

93

highest point, but—he looks at the empty patio, over my head—who could tell what the highest point would be? What could be used as a reference? The past? There was a flood in aught five, in twenty-six, in sixty-two; those were the biggest ones. None of them got up to the same point, they were all different. He falls silent. When they rise, slowly, over months, burying entire provinces beneath dark water, those chaotic rivers take not only our lands, our animals, our trees, but also, and perhaps in a surer and more permanent way, our conversations, our courage, and our recollections. They entomb, they disable our communal memory, our identity. And, although it is cold, the May sun shines down on the empty red metal tables arranged on the patio. There is a sunny silence. There is a fixed green stain, the cashier sitting upon a stool, one hand resting on the lever of the cash register. The murmur of the city, intermittent and continual, comes to me mutedly. Now that I let myself be consumed by the crowd, on the corner by the bank, standing immobile, smoking, I think, unpremeditatedly, about the empty bar in the galleria, about the sunny patio, about the green stain that is the cashier, his hand resting on the lever of the cash register. They will persist, empty, without me. Suddenly, smoothly, standing fifty centimeters from my face, a man, with a rosette in the lapel of his overcoat, clean shaven, about thirty years old, pats my arm, smiling, his head somewhat bent toward me and his green eyes half closed: what am I so pensive about standing on the street corner at eleven o'clock in the morning, although getting a bit of sun is certainly worthwhile. His face is somehow familiar to me. He must be, I think, one of those friends that Cat makes every time he goes on a bender with Tomatis or with Héctor, at the Progress Club or at Copacabana. One of those who thinks that Cat has forgotten about them—Cat never forgets anyone who has spoken two words to him, ever—when they confuse me for him on the street and I receive them coolly. Now he has gone. People pass around me, on the sidewalk and on the street, and when I throw it, my cigarette hits the curb and keeps smoking on the asphalt. Bringing a piece of warm meat to my mouth, in the restaurant, at the same table where I ate yesterday with Héctor, before Héctor's empty chair, among the muffled sounds, I stand still, not suddenly, midway, recalling the shaved face, the green eyes, the gray coat, the lapel: accustomed to his mistake, about to leave, with my suitcase packed beside the bed, the plane ticket, exhausted, I see that failing to recognize the man on the street corner by the bank as the painter Héctor introduced to me, fleetingly, in the restaurant, shows that I can only conceive of being recognized for myself with uncertainty or disbelief. I shake my head, laughing; I swallow the mouthful. The taxi driver stops before reaching the bridge, when the policeman seems to want to come out of the sentry box to signal to him. Vehemently, looking at me from time to time through the rearview mirror, where a fragment of my face appears at one of the angles, the driver, whose bald oval head seems incapable of sitting still for even a moment, has been telling me that the explosions were a faulty measure, proposed by the army, and that now those breaches will stay open for years. I pay him and get out. Until he has seen the car turn around, after two or three laborious maneuvers, and take off down the boulevard, the policeman doesn't look at me. In the siesta sun, a head taller than me, hands held away from his body, dark face below his visor, body covered in the maroon over- coat belted by a bandoleer, legs akimbo, the policeman, because he is far from me, seems more precise, more perfect. He uses not only his gaze, but his whole body to watch the car depart. Now his sparkling boots scrape threateningly as he turns toward me. Yes, there are steamboats and canoes going out to El Rincón. You get off at La Guardia, there is a motorboat pulling a barge, and then, at the entrance to the town, a canoe. Out of habit he stands at attention, unostentatiously, at least it seems to me, when I leave.

The breeze cools the light in the middle of the bridge, a weak platform above the water, which dominates everything, and from which emerge, intermittently, trees, posts, buildings. Below, against the central column, currents, visible on the surface, intertwine, breaking the smoothness of the great liquid expanse, lifting crests that shudder, rugged and foamy, as if around the column there were, so to speak, a deep hole into which all of the water had come to fall. From the bridge, before reaching the other end, I see the Boating Club building, red tiles and white walls, half submerged: water comes and goes through the doors, through the windows. On the other side of the club are a ravine and a narrow path that runs along the water among the trees. Soldiers, people, canoes, and a steamboat are visible. An officer directs the embarkation. There is a strip of dry land thirty feet across and no more than six feet wide. I approach the group, keeping quiet: almost no one speaks. Some have boarded the steamboat. Others prepare to get on. Others watch, as if they weren't going themselves. Suddenly, a telephone rings. I see then that the officer, elated by his job and the general situation, jumps toward the side and plunges his feet into the water, and I can make out, upon a slim, narrow little table, the telephone. With my eyes I follow the cable, which, going over the tops of the trees, disappears into the Boating Club. The officer speaks into the telephone for a moment, his feet sunk in the water. When he's finished, he returns to directing our embarkation. Now, searching blindly, having left the shore, for what, until a few months back, was the path of a stream, we sail, precariously, slowly, crammed into the little steamboat, the rhythm of its motor broken, intermittent, in the middle of the great aquatic expanse from which tall tufts of *paja brava* grass, camalote and, far off, ranches and trees, half flooded, jut forth. Next to one of them I can make out, now almost stripped of paint, the metal of its roof eaten away by rust, a minibus submerged in the water. We get off at the asphalt road. There are people waiting for the steamboat on the shore. The motorboat is nowhere to be seen. When the steamboat's motor cuts so we can dock, and we are slowly approaching the shore, the silence is so great, so vast, that I sense, for a fleeting moment, arduously, completely, growing, the exodus, the general dread, the distress, the death. Touching land, I trip and fall forward. Someone holds me up–there are exclamations and a few laughs. Many of those dark faces, that all look alike, are familiar to me. Some greet me. The majority of those waiting on the shore get onto the steamboat. Soldiers, a non-commissioned officer, direct the embarkation. Off to one side of the dock, hastily reinforced with wood and sheets of zinc, precarious, is a drink stand. Someone says that the motorboat has just left for El Rincón and won't be back for another hour. Others talk about the explosions, the bulletins, the military. An entire family that didn't manage to get onto the steamboat and now stands on the shore, waiting for its return, ask a soldier for information about the encampment at Boca del Tigre. From the way he answers them, vaguely, quickly, indecisively, I sense that the soldier doesn't even know the encampment exists; the totality of a catastrophe is the privilege of its spectators, not its protagonists. At the drink stand I have a gin, between two men speaking in low voices. I buy a bottle for Cat. There is something else I catch, for a moment, in the flavor of that gin drunk in the cool, sinking sun, other than the years I've already lost, other than a certain forgetfulness and a certain immobility, a certain objection, and it is, mixed with the scent of water and the scent of poverty, something invisible and ironclad like a root, food, a preexisting relationship through which my separation is not the division of two distinct parts which coexist, in enmity, inside me, but the end of a marriage to something that, for lack of a better word, I call the world. Needles, as you might say, of gold, still high up, draw lines across the blue sky. Before the motorboat, sending up its weak, regular explosions, arrives, again, full of people, coming slowly to dock, sailing over what used to be a street in La Guardia, fragile, old, the steamboat. With the glass of gin in my hand, I see, from among the group that has crammed onto shore preparing to board, people jumping to the ground. Now I am standing on the barge pulled, laboriously, by the motorboat, and I grab hold of the crosspiece, looking at the fields on either side of the road. Not too high, contained, but demonstrating, nevertheless, through that calm, that it will be the last to withdraw, the water covers the fields, coils around the trunks of trees, hammers, imperceptibly, against walls, bridges, embankments. The asphalt is stained with mud, detritus, debris. In Colastiné, on a relatively elevated point around which the water nibbles tranquilly, there is another encampment. The motorboat stops; children and dogs run from the tents toward the people getting off, and women and men, busy boiling water, chopping wood, interrupt their work a moment to look in the direction of the trailer. Soldiers walk idly among the tents, around which accumulate, in disorder, baubles, blankets, and basins. Then the orange motorboat starts up again, with the driver, who holds his back, covered by a short wool jacket, rigid, before me, and a soldier who accompanies him, standing in the front, his face ruddy from the cold air. All these months I've gotten no impression of any sort of violence from the water, but rather, and even more when its habit of growing had settled down inside us, of discretion, placidity, silence, and I have had to see the people at Boca del Tigre, in Colastiné, in encampments, piled up in front of the slate at *La Region*, talking about the explosions, the bulletins, to perceive, in flashes, like someone coming upon zones, crossing them, and finally leaving them behind, stable, the violence. Now I jump down from the barge, at the entrance to El Rincón; my feet, flexing, stick firmly on the asphalt and I straighten up to contemplate the water covering, with a reddish tinge, the wide, straight road, on whose edges the abandoned houses, made of concrete or adobe, vivid in the sun, still high in the sky, stand half submerged in water. The sun at four, pale, sparkles weakly in a green sky. There is within us, despite the canoes that wait on the shore, against the embankment, despite the tents scattered along the road, around which human figures move, despite all of this and because of the silence, now that the motorboat has stopped and the few voices that can be heard fade away almost instantly, diffused, a sense that, rather than standing before an abandoned town, we have arrived, for the first time and being, moreover, the first ever, in a virgin place, without fauna, submerged in blind water where life has not yet formed. The man from the canoe, who rows in front of me along the submerged road, toward the center of town, swaying back and forth rhythmically, with a cigarette between his lips that has gone out, turning his head every so often to look at the patios entombed underwater, asks me, after a moment of rowing in silence, above the regular splash of his oars that has been the only sound flowing out into the green air before his voice, if I have been in the city or if I have only come from La Guardia, and if I have come just to buy a bottle of gin and go back. I tell him that I'm coming from the city. You got here quick, he responds, incredulous. Then he says they shouldn't have blown away the road: that the soldier had told him yesterday afternoon that the army was preparing the explosions and that he hadn't believed him until he heard them; that he was sleeping in a tent and that he had not only heard the noise but felt, both times, the tremor of the ground where he was lying. He himself, he says, is not from the town but from up north, beyond Leyes, where there's practically no dry land left at all. To San Javier, from the city, he says, you have to go by boat; they've filled in the embankment with sandbags, but the water gets through anyway. Now he is quiet; we proceed through deserted streets, and the oars, hitting the water, bring up a weak crest that opens out toward the shores, more every time, and crashes against the sidewalks, against the fronts of houses; where there are no buildings, the little crest goes through the tissue of wires and loses itself, silently, at the end of patios, among the tree trunks. Turning onto a cross street, I see, through the wide-open door of a house, the water running over the legs of the furniture, and on the wall, beside another door that leads to a room further inside, a mirror, and over it, on the blue wall, a large oval portrait. After turning two or three times, in complete silence, at the height of twilight, toward the outskirts of town, asleep more because of the water and the time of day than because of the rhythm of the oars, not anxious, not euphoric, divided, over the head of a man who leans forward, straightens up a moment and then leans back, growing, coming closer, the only dry point in town even though it is built on the banks of the stream, over the ravine, vivid, compact, its windows open, human vigor emanating from it even though no one is yet visible, separated from the water by many yards of dry land, on a slope, a bit strange to me because of its savage contrast to the landscape, elevated, in the middle, white, enormous, the house. In the cold it looks even whiter, more arid. In front of the door there are some canoes that tremble in the wake that grows larger as we approach the shore and dock. Pushing in the half-open door, I hear, muffled, the slow tapping of a typewriter. Now that I have passed through the first room I see, immediately, by the light of the kerosene lamp, rigid on his chair, contemplating the paper in the typewriter with his hands elevated, about to hit the keys, the figure of Washington, whose white head moves brusquely toward me, unperturbed. He regards me for a moment, fixed, without blinking, as I advance toward the center of the sphere of clarity diffused by the lantern. I thought it was Cat, Washington says, offering me a bony, dry hand, which he takes back in a moment. I ask how he is. You can see for yourself, he says. From the patio comes the cry of a child, a laugh. It's Don

Layo's family, Washington says. Cat has left them behind, the same as him: they didn't want to stay at home and had gotten some tents from the army. We'll lose everything this time, he says, because the whole island is underwater. He's silent. The disappointment of discovering that it is me and not Cat must have mixed itself within him with the feeling that I am an intruder, simply because, to his eyes, my love, my veneration, which may have been, in other times, greater than Cat's, have the defect of not being Cat's. He lowers his eyes, playing with the cold *mate* on top of the table. Cat, he tells me circumspectly, has gone to the city, to see me: he'll be back at six. But six is also when the last motorboat leaves for La Guardia, where it meets with the last steamboat. I tell him to keep working, I'll wait. I regard him fleetingly, two or three times, while he writes on the typewriter. Now he's sitting in the chair. No longer is he like the last time I saw him, in November, on the patio of his house, a *mate* in his hand, standing next to Cat and Tomatis, talking about the fundamentals of Tendai, beneath the hot sun, against a background, fresh and flowering, of birds of paradise and laurels. Now he is seated before me. The keys of the machine resound, pounding against the white sheet, in an atmosphere of circumspection. He is, facing me with his white head, his dry face, the color of earth, despite his wool shirt with large red and white checks beneath whose half-open collar peeps a woolen undershirt, despite the invisibility of the time that he has lived, or perhaps more than anything because of it, in which he has been a child, an adolescent, an adult, despite his multiple lives, sitting before the typewriter, without glasses, tidy, extravagant, an old man. Voices keep coming rapidly, in bursts, from the patio, and when the typewriter stops and Washington sits with his hands suspended in the air, over the keyboard, his gaze fixed on the piece of paper, they sound louder, sharper. Now I am standing on the balcony out back, seeing the tents scattered on the patio, among the trees, and among them a bonfire, whose tallest flames are even taller than the tents, spreads a reddish splendor in the still-bright air. Don Layo has greeted me, among the tumult of his nephews and the women who are preparing pots and kettles around the fire. Then he disappeared inside one of the tents. Five or six dogs prowl in the background, behind the tents which are separated from the balcony by a great expanse of open terrain where there are not even trees, in which are strewn car batteries half-buried in the ground among the yellowing grass, the tips of which has been singed by the cold. Men, tents, trees, mixed up, extinguishing themselves with the day, are enveloped and cushioned by a lilac twilight, now that I have gone out again with the glass of gin in my hand to pass along the balcony I hear, faintly, with momentary pauses and new starts, intermittent, weak, hesitant, the tapping of the typewriter that comes, in bursts, from inside the house. Our two shadows project, silently, against the white wall, enormous. He has just said that Cat, unless by exceptional means, won't be coming. For him to manage it, there would have to be the possibility, utterly remote, of obtaining permission from the police or the army to cross the suspension bridge, by foot, at night, and the possibility, afterward, of some embarkation from the Boating Club to La Guardia, and furthermore of walking from La Guardia to the entrance to El Rincón, and managing to find someone to bring him in a canoe from the entrance of town to the house, in the middle of the night, which would oblige one, like it or not, to dismiss the idea that he could be coming back tonight. He takes a large sip of gin, a shorter one, leaves the glass on the table, slips a cigarette, deliberately, into the black mouthpiece, bites down on it, tasting it a little with his lips while he searches for the matches on the table, lights the cigarette, draws a mouthful of smoke, drops the matches back onto the table and, pulling the mouthpiece between his teeth, supporting it over the edge of the table and waving his hand in front of his face to disperse the smoke, smiles briefly and adds that if everything indicates he won't come now, it may very well turn out the opposite, because with Cat, I know quite well from experience, you just never know. Now I am sitting before the typewriter, my hands held above the keyboard, waiting for Washington to dictate to me. If, as I hear his voice and bend over quickly, pounding the keys with the pads of my fingers, someone were to enter, seeing us, without knowing, from the door-frame, holding his hand out to greet us, affable, he would believe, and would continue to believe if we didn't reveal his error, that I, leaning over the keyboard, was someone else. And I myself, at the moment I begin to type, emptied of prejudice, of spite, of fear, of indifference, dedicated simply to writing, suspend myself, erasing myself, without being myself, and having, for a moment, if not the possibility of being someone else, the certainty, at least, of being no one, nothing, just as I am not the sentences that come from Washington and pass through me, from my arms, exit through the tips of my fingers and imprint themselves, in pairs, on the paper sitting in the machine. The smoke from our cigarettes is filling up the sphere of light radiating from the lamp, and from outside, no noises, no voices come to us, nor the horizon of animal sounds, polyphonic, that the water forces, so to speak, according to Washington, toward the dry border, where they are stored. There is nothing, now that Washington, absorbed in the translation that he is dictating to me, thinks neither of me nor of Cat, but only about the sentences that he polishes with his gazed fixed on his notebook while he wrinkles his forehead and arches, reflectively, his white brow, nothing but my conviction, extremely weak, my impover-ished certainty, to corroborate the idea that I have not been here all day, sitting before the typewriter copying Washington's transla-tion, and that rather I only arrived here a few hours ago, on a boat, on an orange motorboat, on a canoe. I have just conserved, weakly, mixed up, diffused, the little flame burning, that now, suddenly, at the moment when I return to re-reading, at Washington's request, a sentence I have already written, when my attention is displaced, insignificant, dies out. I end up thinking that the two of us are outside of something, something that has bid us goodbye, leaving us outside and closing the door behind us at the edge of darkness, even when we are perhaps the only ones, in the darkest point of a night replete with water, who are exposed in full light, arid and slow, as if under observation. I am not in that exteriority; although he is absent, Cat is there. Now Washington dictates to me: A good laborer   a good laborer   does not make with a needle   more than   with a needle a good laborer does not make more than five stitches per minute comma   more than five stitches per minute comma   per minute comma   while certain circular machines   While certain circular weaving machines   make thirty thousand in the same time period   Every minute of machine work   every minute of machine work   Every minute of machine work is equal   therefore   Every minute of machine work is equal therefore to a hundred hours of work by a laborer semicolon   or rather every minute of work   or rather every minute of machine work allows the laborer   permits the laborer   ten days of rest period   ten days of rest period   Now I am walking behind Washington, who carries the lantern, with the bottle of gin and the glasses, following him in the direction of the kitchen, behind the swinging lantern that produces continuous, irregular movements of light and shadow all around, crossing two of the large white rooms, practically empty. Now Washington cuts an onion into fine slices on the stove while I am peeling, a cigarette hanging between my lips, potatoes that now I begin to dry and cut into slices so I can throw them into the oil that crackles in the black saucepan, over the fire. Born from the belly of a woman, fed by two great white tits and sheltered by a firm skirt against the broad belly of his mother in the years of his infancy, obsessed during his adolescence with the delirium of women's bodies, married, divorced, then both again, father of a daughter, frequenter of prostitutes at sixty, surrounded by women like a stamen surrounded by petals, Washington does not seem, now, leaning over the stove, as he slices the onion, either androgynous or hermaphroditic but asexualized, as if the floodgates of sex had closed for him, in him, and now there were a pair of old people living together at the end, tranquil, reconciled, at the same time, in the same body. And eating, now, separated by the bread and the bottle of wine, I see, firmly, his age. He chews slowly, erect, ascetic, never allowing his rough, wrinkled hands, or his lined mouth to be stained or shine with oil. He condescends to speak, even though I am not Cat. He holds his glass of wine in the air, chewing, serious, and affirms: to travel, you will see, is to pass from the particular to the universal, and as one travels the particular turns into the universal, and the universal, the particular; they do nothing, that is, but switch places. Now he is setting the lamp on the table, next to the typewriter. I contemplate him; I can, if I like, he says, sleep, though it will only be a few hours, in Cat's bed; Don Layo, in the morning, will take me to the road. From the bed I hear the typewriter, in the other room. On the table the light burns, tranquil, a lamp; it doesn't even flicker. Lying face-up as I smoke, I extend, without looking, my hand toward the nightstand and pick up the tall glass of gin. I sit up and take a sip. Now there is no more noise from the typewriter. Nothing is audible. Hearing nothing, one knows that one is within the black point of the present, a grain of sand, so to speak, in the lunar sphere, the black point of the present that is as long and as wide as time itself, in someone else's bed. And now in the sun, in the back hall, I see boys playing against the tents and the smoke, while I listen to Don Layo chewing his *mate*, one foot propped up on a half-buried car battery: they have said, yes, about the explosions; as far as the island, everything is underwater.

A black dog jumps two or three times in front of the old man, and then stands on his hind legs. Don Layo refills the *mate* and offers it to me. Washington comes out of the house, with his own *mate* and another straw. I end up between the two old men who talk, tranquilly, about a catastrophe that, in one sense, doesn't even graze them, me, who flees from it practically trembling. Two old men who speak serenely, respectfully, who have had time, paying for it with their years, to get to this point and in which, surrounded by water that is rising, and that will continue to rise, are standing, firm, polished, like bones, drinking *mate* in the cold sunlight of the morning, warmer, paradoxically, than at noon. Still, they offer, so to speak, no lesson. They offer nothing. More exterior than the house, the trees, the smoke, and more fleeting, they extract, even for themselves, no conclusion. Now I watch Washington suck the *mate*, put the silver tube in his mouth, sip, and sip for him, in him, while Don Layo, watching him, waiting, offers me the full *mate* again. I sip, in turn, from the other *mate*. Go take a look at the Federalists' Wall when you get there, he tells me, at the door, as I am getting into the canoe. I tell him that I will go. Say hello to your mother for me, Don Layo tells me, when he leaves me at the road. And then, again, in an inverse sense, standing in the barge being pulled, slowly, by the orange motorboat, I retrace the path, seeing how, helplessly, dark, among the children, the dogs, the smoke, the tents slip away. And then: La Guardia under water, the bridge, the city. I cross, so to speak, a fixed place that I believe, because I am traveling, will stay behind. In the galleria, Elisa, in a blue dress, sits at a table on which there are two small cups, both empty. He went back to El Rincón, she tells me. I sit down in front of one of the cups; Elisa is sitting in front of the other. They went around look-ing for you, with Tomatis, she says. She looks at me. She thinks, even so, that I am not Cat. I ask myself what he has to go to El Rincón for, she says. Washington is with him, I say. In the silence that follows, monotonous, the proprietor's voice comes from behind the counter, speaking with the cashier. Héctor's elastic face, behind his pipe, appears in the corridor of the galleria, and when he sits with us, Héctor, after thumping me twice softly on the shoulder, asks after Cat: someone, he says, told him that he saw him around here yesterday. He returned this morning. He must have come to say goodbye to me, I say. Elisa says that she must get the boys when school gets out. Héctor gives her the keys. I don't think I'll be able to come to the station tonight, says Elisa, standing up. I feel, for the last time, against my arid cheek, her own, smooth, fleeting when I stand and brush, as a goodbye, my left cheek against her right cheek, after having brushed, quickly, for a fraction of a second, my right cheek against her left. Héctor is watching me as I remain standing, seeing her pass through the glass door, enter the corridor, disappear among the illuminated places, thinking, imprecisely, vaguely, that it is not love that awakens nostalgia, but, more mechanically, the experience, the perception, the familiarity even with that which rejects us, going around us, inert. Now the two of us are standing in the sun, on the sidewalk, the pipe that juts out of his elastic face emitting a weak column of smoke among the people who pass and who, inattentive, must change directions to pass the part of the sidewalk we intercept with our bodies. Now, after having rejected his invitation to go to lunch, saying I have mountains of things to get done at home, after having said goodbye until tonight at the station, I cross the sunny street, make it to the other side, walk through the murmur of the city as if submerged in a transparent river, dull, continuous, in the direction of my house. Now I am in the bedroom, standing between the two beds, seeing Cat's, slept in, and mine, made up. On my pillow there is a note: I couldn't find you anywhere. You shouldn't have gone to El Rincón. We were looking for you, me and Tomatis. What about the explosions? Come back soon because out there you will find nothing.

Send me your address so I can write to you right away. Hugs. Cat. One more thing: Since we didn't have enough time to pay the bill— we ate at El Tropezón—I signed your name. Don't worry, Tomatis will drop by to take care of it. More hugs. Now I am looking at the white municipal building through the window. It is immersed, so to speak, in the blue sky. I have come this morning from El Rincón, I have been with Elisa and with Héctor in the bar in the galleria, I have walked home, I have been in the bedroom seeing Cat's disheveled bed and my intact one, I have read the note he left for me on the pillow, and now I am standing beside the desk, looking through the window at the white municipal building that shines in the noon sun and is immersed, so to speak, in the blue sky. Chewing with difficulty, slowly, listening to my vague story about Don Layo's family and the submerged island, without much effort, my mother, younger than her salt-and-pepper hair, which gives her the air of a mature actress made up to play an old woman on television, conceals, beneath a thin patina of resignation, a certain indifference. A kind of tiredness prevents her from showing more effusion. We are delivered from this embarrassment, suddenly, by the telephone. The maid comes to say that it is for me. I am still swallowing when I pick up the earpiece and hear Tomatis's voice. It, he says, is sinking. It is sinking. It keeps rising. Tonight they will blow up more of the embankments. The ones who are leaving are right to go. I tell him that I have been to El Rincón to see Cat and that Cat, on the other hand, had come to eat in the city with the rest of the tramps. Tomatis laughs: he had suggested to him, he says, that I might have gone to El Rincón. Well, Pigeon, says Tomatis, for the last time: give up this absurd trip! I promise, if you do, to wash away your sins with water, so much water. Your limitations, I say, are the same as the Devil's: temptation is your only power. The only real power, says Tomatis: the rest is pure demagoguery. He too, will be at my sendoff, that's why he's called, he says, tonight, at ten to twelve, at

the bus station, and between the end of his sentence and the sound
of the operator cutting the line, there is a silence, a vacillation,
something imprecise, as if his voice, already faint, were trying
fruitlessly, indecisively, to say something and not at all to rectify, to
distance himself, to console himself, but simply, almost mechanically, to continue talking a bit, to fill, with a pause, the duration,
which is not more than a moment, in which his voice, fragmentary,
sticks, just like my mother now, just now, delaying the end of dinner, offers me dessert, an orange, a coffee, to stick something clear,
precise, formal, to the unmediated duration that, if you like, is no
longer than a moment but as wide, even so, as time itself. Now the
two of us are standing before the steel blue light of the television,
seeing the bulletin. It is rising, and will continue to rise, says the
bulletin. We see soldiers evacuate, to the north, an entire village:
cots, blankets, heaters, animals, children pass by, precariously, in
trailers, in trucks, are outlined, in single file, on the embankments,
surrounded by water, against a background of naked trees and
ranches in ruins, half submerged in water. Taken from the air, we
see, on the coast, a strip that clearer and almost imperceptibly more
serene than the two great plains that hem it in, the breaches in the
embankment, and, beside the first, almost flattened against the
pavement and the rubble, a black car and two human figures. After
the image fades I recognized myself, retrospectively, standing next
to Héctor as he contemplates, leaning over, the water flowing from
the breaches. Now they show the breaches again, empty, always
from above, and the image advances, devouring the road, the water,
leaving it behind, until the tips of the towers of the suspension
bridge come into view, its platform, seen from above, seeming level
with the water; at the mouth of the bridge, heading out slowly
toward the boulevard, a black car—us—and the first houses. I get
up, intercepting, for a moment, the steel blue image. Slowly I cross
the anteroom, the bedroom, and I see, from the window, the steel

blue image, showing, flattened, from above, beside the breaches, two human figures, Héctor and me. Then I lay down and smoke, in silence, with the ashtray on my chest as I look at, without seeing, the ceiling. Strictly speaking, I think for fifteen minutes, while I smoke, about nothing. I am, so to speak, the center, the white wall, where images undulate like flags. Now I am passing again before the flickering steel blue screen, intercepting, for a moment, with my body, my mother's vision as she fidgets, slightly annoyed, in her seat. Standing now, fixed, I am once again looking at the white municipal building immersed, so to speak, in the blue sky. An exceptionally small man, visible only from the waist up, walks in the sun, on the terrace, half of him erased by a white wall. He leans on it a moment and looks down. It is easier, like that, at a distance, to be standing, looking down, no vertigo, no memories, with the cold wind that should be blasting up there—more so since the light has begun to fade—in bursts, on his cheeks. He is relaxed, compact against the sky. Nothing at all seems to rise, from his toes to his head, nor does there rise, toward his muscles, his skin, the unstable, continuous murmur of his entrails working, complex, in the dark. He advances, perfect, opaque, indestructible, half of a dark figure emerging from the white wall, in the terrace, and now that I turn toward my desk he disappears, becoming a new memory that I carry with me and that begins to descend, like food, toward the combustion engine of memory that chews it, mixes it, polishes it, stores it in a great mobile enclosure in which all things, though they may change size and place, remain. From the third drawer in the desk, which is open, I am taking out reams of paper, tearing them up without looking at them and dropping them into the trash. I do that for half an hour. I look out, once in a while, at the flowerpots in the narrow patio, blocked off by the yellow walls. And now once again my body is intercepting the flickering steel blue image, in the room through which afternoon advances getting colder and darker. Her arms crossed over her chest, her salt and pepper hair, too smooth and well combed and parted to seem natural, immobile and half standing in the direction of the flickering image, my mother asks, distractedly, without listening for my laconic affirmative response, if I have everything ready. Now I am adjusting the collar of my overcoat as I go slowly down the stairs. When I open the door, the homogeneous murmur of the city becomes more varied and stronger than what had been coming to me as I descended, adjusting, unhurriedly and ineffectually, the collar of my coat. Innumerable, the city embraces me. It is more than the straight, gray sidewalks I walk along, more than the shop windows, diverse and packed with things, that flank me, than the people who come walking in the opposite direction on the same sidewalk, on the opposite sidewalk, who pass beside me, brushing me lightly, who cross the street, who stand before the shop windows and the cigarette kiosks, who watch me pass from inside the bars, who pass by driving cars, more than yellow, white, gray houses, one or two stories tall, and the bus and the cars that pile up on the main streets and wait for the signal of the traffic guard, their motors running, more than the sounds, the neighborhoods, the smells, more even than the memories interwoven in a common space that, even so, is not the same one where our bodies pass, more than the empty spaces, the water that rises, slowly, surrounding it, more than the opaque material that is always before our eyes and nevertheless refracts our memory, through which I advance, moving my arms and legs as if I were swimming, with my eyes open, in an ocean of stone. In a city without memory, those who remember, in your streets, direct like destinies, erroneous, fateful, they are mistaken, I formulate, attempting, fruitlessly, to memorize it as I arrive, walking slowly, at the bus station. In your straight streets—amended—continuous like rays, erroneous, fateful, they are mistaken. I pass through garages stained with oil, passing among the great yellow and red buses. Loudspeakers blare, confused, urgent. There are mountains of suitcases around the cigarette kiosks and newsstands. I argue for some minutes, leaning in front of the hole in the ticket window and manage, at last, urged discretely by the impatient line, to change my ticket. And now I am again, the cigarette smoke mixing into the weakest, most transparent of coffees, standing in front of the counter of the bar in the galleria, with my back to the full patio on which the cold clarity of the end of the afternoon falls monotonously, and already I am going up to the cashier in green overalls, the pads of whose tidy fingers brush the palm of my hand at the moment he returns my 100 pesos change. Those who remember, I settle on, at last, listless, weak, knowing that I will forget it, in your streets, direct like destinies, erroneous, fateful, they are mistaken. And now I am again climbing the stairs of my house, getting free of my coat, intercepting again with my body, for a moment, the steel blue image that flickers in the room, even darker, perceiving again, as I pass, my mother's white head that nods a moment, to one side, losing no time to recover the image that I have blocked. Now the suitcase and the blue bag, on the bed. I see, through the window, on the sidewalk out front, repeated six times, in two rows of three, one on top of the other, the face of a man who speaks and then of a rapid cut, also repeated six times, to another face, its head covered by a military cap. I stand for a moment to listen as I am passing from the bedroom to the library: it is a colonel informing the populace: it is rising, and will continue to rise. They are evacuating Boca del Tigre, Barranquitas. There will be more explosions. And then, mutely, the images start up: military trucks advancing, darkly, down an avenue, turning on cross streets, in a monotonous convoy that divides, coming to a corner, into two files going in opposite directions; a great expanse of water from which emerge, half covered, feeble ranches; military tents set up on an enormous fallow field, among which a few women gathered in a circle, dressed in black, speak with two soldiers; once again, in detail, moving with a regular rhythm, chewing away at the border of an embankment, which has been reinforced with sandbags, firm, placid, the water. And again, from the air, the clearest strip of road between two interminable expanses and beside the breaches in the embankment, a little closer than the black abandoned car in the middle of the road, with its doors open, two figures, irreconcilable, flattened, and immediately, also from above, the tips of the towers of the suspension bridge and its platform, from whose edge, at the entrance to the city, Héctor's black car slowly goes out and, with some maneuvering, heads onto the boulevard. Other images accompany me spontaneously when I come, perhaps for the last time, to the desk and sit, looking out at the patio surrounded by the yellow walls and at the flowerpots whose ferns have already begun to be erased, spreading out into the twilight: the arid, white house, in the January sun, and the river, from which Cat comes spouting water, passing, narrowly, golden, toward the south; Washington talking, when the smoke from his cigarette rises in the sun, about the fundamentals of Tendai—first proposition: the world is unreal; second proposition: the world is a transitory phenomenon; third proposition, and pay attention, this is the fundamental one: the world is neither unreal nor a transitory phenomenon—close to Cat and Tomatis, against a background, fresh and flowered, of birds of paradise and laurels; and last, mobile, harmonious: Cat, freshly bathed, descending the stairs in shirtsleeves, a drop of water falling from the hair stuck to his sunburned forehead, the smell, crude and savage, of the river still impregnating his body, stronger than the soap and the summer, coming afterward, so identical to me that he waves two or three times, from one sidewalk to the other, at some men who have confused him for me, on one corner in the city where he stands, smoking. It is not, I formulate, I realize, either love, or nostalgia, or any elemental cause that calls forth these brilliant images, but rather the mystery of time, of space, its inert, dense, solid operations, purer and clearer, more real than our own weak adhesion, I formulate, like the shadow, speckled with light, of a tree over the river. More embattled, stronger, the streets, the houses, yellow and gray, walls, on the foundation of the planet, in the mornings, in the afternoons, should not leave, so to speak, a greater trace than the time they are made of, toward the outside, for no one, constant, blind, refractory, occasionally wetted by the pendulum of the rain, regularly charred by the swing to summer, now that I stand up in the darkness and go, silently, to the kitchen to watch the steam rise, in front of my mother at the other side of the table, from my bowl of soup. We hardly talk, separated by a white and green checkered tablecloth, the bread cut in two, the tureen that shines in the light of the lamp and steams, the half-full bottle of wine and two full cups, the thick white crockery plates, the meat, the pepper, the oil, the oranges, the salt. Only when I tell her that I have changed my ticket, that I will go at ten instead of at midnight, does she shake, without effusion, her salt-and-pepper head, too well-kept to seem natural, hiccup two or three times, and burst into tears. Her cry is only a couple seconds long, flushing her face and passing immediately. And now I am putting on my overcoat, adjusting the collar, picking up the bag and the suitcase, having said goodbye, slowly going down the stairs and arriving on the street just in time to see three military trucks, in a line, coming from the darkness, pass under the light at the corner, identically, slowly, and go on to be enveloped into the darkness of the next block. I think about nothing, I formulate nothing. And it is not them, on the other hand, the streets, the corners, the signs, all of which remain behind me as I walk toward the station, receding, but me, more precisely, who is erased, gradually, from these corners, these streets. The green bus waits, half empty, illuminated inside, on the platform. At the newsstand I buy *La Región:* It is rising and will continue to rise. Among the others there is a blurry photograph, taken from the air, of the breaches in the embankment: the great white expanses, the slightly darker strip upon which a black car is visible, its doors open, as if abandoned, and beside the breaches—an uneven fringe of arid blackness—two flattened figures, dressed in black. Just when I put my foot on the step, my right foot on the step, my left hand holding the blue bag into which I have put the paper, from far away, I hear the explosion. The glass and the metal shake, briefly, on the bus. Walking down the aisle, I pass, so to speak, through a murmur of discrete commentary, looking for my seat. There is still a vague echo of the explosion in my head. There is no memory, it is still too fresh to be more than a residue, already extremely thin, of perception. And now, the illuminated bus starts up, slowly, leaves, so to speak, because it's me who is above, leaving behind the station, the streets of the city, like a node of lights, red, green, blue, yellow, violet, the corners, the coupled houses, monotonous, one or two stories tall, the parks crisscrossed by the darkness, the humble avenues, the neighborhoods scattered among the trees, the city that closes itself off like a sphincter, like a circle, bidding me farewell, leaving me outside, further outside of her than of my mother's womb, and she herself further outside, with all of her men, and her memories, and the passion of all of her men that mixes together, even so, in a zone that coexists, higher up, on level with the stones. We stop, before reaching the checkpoint, behind a file of military trucks. On the other side of the avenue is the soccer stadium, and closer up, in the enormous open space that separates the stadium from the avenue, the tents erected in disorder, darker than the frozen night that envelopes them and lower than the point of the bonfires that burn, scattered, in the clearings and that form an arid, mobile circle of yellow light in the darkness. The light inside the bus goes out:

someone, *something* contemplates, or, more accurately, looks at, or, more accurately, *sees*, through the cold glass, the garbage heap, the wide winter, the mute tents, the bonfires, and some anonymous shadows that move around the fire, piles of objects without names, stored in disorder, bodies, denser, like the tents, than the night, but taller, sometimes, than the flames, cross the black open air that must be impregnated with the smell of water, and in which must flutter, at times, with the sound of flames, the broken canvas of the tents and the murmur of the trucks, and the crystal of the frost and the cries of the beasts accumulated on the narrow fringes of the still-firm earth. We start up. The second explosion goes off. I enter Boca del Tigre.

The One Before

Earlier, others could. They would wet, slowly, in the kitchen, in the afternoon, in the winter, the cookie, soaking it, and raise, afterward, their hands, in a single movement, to their mouths, they would bite it and leave, for a moment, the sugared dough on the tip of their tongues, so that from it, from its dissolution, like dew, memory would rise, they would chew it slowly, and now suddenly they would be outside themselves, in another place, clinging to, for as long as there remained, in the first place, the tongue, the cookie, the steaming tea, the years: they would wet, in the kitchen, in the winter, the cookie in the cup of tea, and they knew, immediately, when they tasted it, that they were full, inside of something and carrying, inside, something, that they had, in other years, because there *were* years, abandoned, outside, in the world, something that could be, in one way or another, so to speak, recovered, and that there was, therefore, somewhere, what they called or what they believed ought to be—isn't it?—a world. And now, I bring to my mouth, for the second time, the cookie soaked in tea and from it I take, tasting it, nothing, what is called nothing. I soak the cookie in the cup of tea, in the kitchen, in the winter, and raise my hand, quickly, to my mouth, I leave the sugared dough, warm, on the tip of my tongue, for a moment, and I begin to chew, slowly, and now that I am swallowing, now that there is not even a trace of flavor, I know, definitively, that I take nothing, absolutely nothing, what is called nothing. Now there is nothing, not even a trace, not even a memory of flavor: nothing. The florescent light, flickering imperceptibly, plunges into and pulls out from darkness, alternately, in the afternoon, the kitchen. I stand, with the cup in my hand, and step out into the blue semidarkness. It is cold and scintillating. The stairs are there, bare, going up to the terrace. Now I am moving forward, in the blue air, on the terrace, and in the blue semidarkness, up above, in the sky, is the moon. The great yellow circle begins, so to speak, to sparkle. And in the blue semidarkness, from the center of the open terrace, the roofs, the terraces, the illuminated windows, the apartment buildings, the six o'clock murmur that rises, monotonous, from the streets, as I go, with the cup in my hand, toward my room. Now I am sitting before the table, the empty cup beside my hands resting on top of the green folder where it says, in red ink, in large, printed letters, PARANATELLON. I am immobile: one hand resting on the other, on top of the closed green folder, where it says, in red ink, in irregular, hurried, large printed letters, PARANATELLON. The empty cup to one side, next to the folder, against a background of piled-up books, of papers, and a glass full of pencils, fountain pens, ballpoints. And on the yellow wall, raising my head, framed by four black bars, inside four wide white margins, the *Wheatfield with Crows*. I think of nothing, what is called nothing. And I remember nothing: no vapor rises—from where?—nothing. Nor am I anywhere else: it is always, now, the same, cold, with the piled-up books, and the papers, and the *Wheatfield with Crows,* place. I am existing, always, now, in the same, with the empty cup and my hands crossed over the PARANATELLON, on the table, place. And now I am standing, I am going through the terrace, black now, among the light fixtures that sparkle, in a circle, around me, from the roofs and the windows and the terraces that have been erased, seeing the round, cold, hard moon that shines, unwavering, in the sky. In the sky at seven, in winter, is, cold, round, shining unwaveringly, I have said, the moon. And I have said that earlier, others could, they would wet, slowly, in the afternoon, in the kitchen, in the winter, the cookie, and would raise, afterward, their hands, from the cup of tea to their mouths, leaving the sugared dough, for a moment, on the tip of their tongues, and immediately—and from where?—there ascended, like a vapor, memory. And I have said: that I would leave the kitchen behind, I would enter the blue air and go up, the cup in my hand, the stairs. With the cup in my hand: the stairs. There was, in the sky at six, hard, brilliant, unwavering, the moon. And I have said: that the florescent, light, flickering imperceptibly, would plunge into and pull out, alternately, entirely, from the darkness, the kitchen. Now I am existing at the edge of the staircase, in the cold, dark air of eight: and now I am existing on the last stair, I am existing on the second to last stair, I am existing on the third to last stair now. On the fourth to last now. And now I am existing on the first stair. I have said that others, in another, so to speak, place, would wet, for a moment, in the cup of tea, the cookie, would bring it, in an instant, to their mouths, letting it rest for a moment on the tip of their tongues, and would begin, then, to drain, so to speak, from the dense block, years, because there would have been, still, for them, or in them, years, and I have said that I used to be going up, afterward, with the cup in my hand, the stairs, that I used to be crossing, in the blue semidarkness, the terrace, that I looked at, alternately, the cold moon, the clear lights, whirling, immobile, in place, around the roofs, the black patios, the terraces, and that, later, I used to be looking at the yellow, blue, green, black, grayish stains, framed, with a lot of white, inside black bars, that before a disorderly background of papers, of books, there used to be the empty cup, my hands crossed over the green folder, beneath the hurried, irregular letters in red ink, that said PARANATELLON, that I used to be existing, first on the last stair, on the second to last, on the third to last, on the fourth to last, on the first stair, on the patio, going again, with the empty cup, to the kitchen that is plunged into and pulled out, again and again, in place, imperceptibly, like everything else, from the darkness. The flow from the tap falls upon the empty cup, and the steaming water spills over. From the living room come the television's peculiar voices, and amplifying them, from below, or more precisely from above, or behind, if you will, in bursts, the music. As one. The cold, fibrous meat and the bread from this morning, mashed, mixed, pass, in pieces, down my throat. The black wine dissolves them and pushes them down, toward the bottom. They must be, in the darkness, one after the other, descending. They must be depositing on the bottom, where mechanisms must have started, already, to work. And when I stand, the food, which is already a memory, stays, in another, so to speak, and in the one where I am still existing, and that should, nevertheless, be the same, place. Now I am existing on the first stair, in the darkness, in the cold. Now I am existing on the second stair. On the third stair now. Now I am existing on the second to last stair. Now I was or I am still existing on the first stair and I was or I am still existing on the first and the second stair and I was or I am existing, now, on the third stair, and I was or I am existing now on the first and on the second and on the fourth and on the seventh and on the third to last and on the last stair. No. I was first on the first stair, then I was on the second, then I was on the third stair, then I was on the third to last, then I was on the second to last, and now I am existing on the last stair. No. I was and I am existing. I was, I was in the midst of being, I am existing, I am in the midst of being, and I am now, having been being, being now on the empty blue terrace, over which shines, round, cold, the moon. Immobile, in the sky, smooth, erasing, around it, the stars, and before me, and refractory, in its way, flat, imaginary, just a name, a word, the moon. In the icy bedroom, I turn on the light. On the table, against a disorganized background of books, of papers, to one side of the glass full of pencils, of ballpoint pens, red, black, green, blue, the green folder, closed, on whose cover I am writing, in large, hurried, nervous letters, with red ink, PARANATELLON. And on the wall, above the desk, with a lot of white around it, behind glass, the *Wheatfield*–but is it really a field? Is it really of wheat?–*with Crows*, and one could, honestly, ask oneself if they are, honestly, crows. They are, more accurately, stains, chaotic blue, yellow, green, black, stains that get more chaotic the closer one gets, stains, a stain, imprecise, that is called a stain, and just as well, because otherwise it would be impossible to know what is, or is not, part of every-thing: a limit. And the flame of the match I bring, carefully, toward the cigarette hanging from my lips, undulates, a stain, yellow and blue, mobile, and stretches, then re-forms, when I blow on it, sev-eral times, before it goes out. The smoke rises, in the bedroom, immobile. It continues, so to speak, to diffuse. In the illuminated air, arabesques and engravings, and a fine vapor, grayish now, hang suspended, especially around the lamp. Down below they must be hearing, in the living room, the television's peculiar voices, and behind them, and below, or around, if you will, intermittent, the music. Intermittent, the television's peculiar voices, they must be hearing, down below, in the living room, that is another, with the flickering bluish light, the two of them sitting in the chairs since the afternoon, in the semidarkness, place. As, into the ashtray, on the table, I tap my cigarette, the smoke makes everything tremble, coming apart. Because earlier, others, so to speak, could: from a round, unpolished face, with a dimple, just one, on the right cheek, from eyes, and from a forehead where black hair, brushed back, springs forth, from the wide mouth, open, or closed, they were able, projecting out, to take some signal, some message, some evi-dence or, even better, a certainty, like, so to speak, a diamond in the rough. From one signal to the next, from a message, or from a certainty, they would cast out, so to speak, lines, and they would put down, in the world, like a mother giving birth, into space, solid, visible, external, or like a dove, in the air, flying, imaginary, in the emptiness, irrefutable, a construction that would serve: a measurement that, simply by existing, would slice up, take apart, classifying, dividing into front, back, after, before, above, below, now, the vague, wandering, continuous stain, identical at every point, without a center, and darker, less defined, without a limit. No message, for me, from this dimple, that appears, with laughter, alone, on the right cheek, no certainty to take: nothing. And the smoke from the cigarette that I take, at this moment, from between my lips, rises, deliberately, intact, toward the ceiling. There should be being around me—illuminated, cold, the straight and deserted streets that intersect every hundred yards, constant—the city. Around me, concentric, squeezing me, like rings, the throng of houses, in one of whose rooms, in each, the same image flickers, bluish, errantly brushing the expressionless, empty faces, changing, organized, manifest, on the television: clusters of given worlds, inside of one, more arduous, that never manifests. They must be about to be, as, toward the ceiling, deliberately, the blue smoke rises, around me, undivided, the city, like a wagon, so to speak, traveling—on what road? and toward what?—in black space. They must be hearing, in each room, in the semidarkness, the voices, and above, or behind, intermittent, the music. The same, for each one, and different, for all the others, and just one, and the same one, for no one, with every one and each one of the rooms, and every one and each one of the steely lights flickering, place: clusters of given worlds, the houses, the trees, the terraces, the streets that intersect every hundred yards, the buildings bleached, like bones, by the moon, the black parks, the rivers, the dirty bars, still open, the murky silhouettes of the last passersby who become easier to make out as they cross, diagonally, below the hanging streetlight, at the corner, the occasional buses, half empty, that, illuminated, go roaring down the avenues, the glass of their windows clouded over with frost, the trash bins waiting, in the cold, for morning, the cars that can be heard suddenly, far away, the streets of the city center, more brilliant, for a moment, than the others, the entire stony collection set inside another, more arduous, that never manifests. And my hand, stubbing out, in the ashtray, on the table, the cigarette, shakes itself out, naked, rough, the skin full of cracks, the nails smooth, pink, trimmed, the hand that has touched, again and again—and when?— with its wrinkled fingers, the dimple, the hand that, having touched the dimple, again and again, has touched, so to speak, nothing, has taken, from the contact, nothing, neither experience, nor certainty, nor a message, nor a sign, nor a memory: nothing. Nothing, unless it might be, fluctuating, the belief that something, slightly higher up, on my forehead and behind it, imaginatively, bottomless, black, flashes, sometimes, from certain bodies, fleetingly, emotions, memories, pleasure, desire, despair, hunger. Nothing that would fall outside of those galaxies, outside of the huge black space without form, without feeling, without direction, with nothing but the wandering ebb and flow, from those phosphorescent flashes, from that brilliance that streaks past, leaving behind a burning tail that is erased, gradually, in time, by the emptiness, or that emerge, from the bottom, if there is, so to speak, a bottom, that sparkle, for a moment, and then, in the same silence, with the same deliberation, without leaving a trace, fade away, flickers of red, green, yellow, wandering violet, white, whose message no one, though they might scrutinize, attentively, that stellar map, can, so to speak, capture— because they say, and there can be said about them, nothing and nothing. The glimmers that sometimes flash, hurriedly, unexpectedly, outside, like sighs, like a voice, like laughter, do not come, perhaps, from that swamp, from that stain. They come, simply, from outside, from the membrane that separates out, so to speak, from the infinite, the real. My hand, which has been known to pass, in other times, without leaving or receiving a trace, comes from the dimple and passes, warm, over my face. For a moment, everything is erased: the yellow wall, the table with the ashtray and the books, with the green folder on which must be written, in red, irregular printed letters, PARANATELLON, the stains crisscrossed with black, with white, the blue, yellow, black stains, the floating smoke, the light, the bookshelf. Everything in the galaxy is confused, startled, and remains trembling for a moment when my hand slides along, gripping at, the membrane. And as my hand heads slowly, to reunite, over my abdomen, with its mate, the galaxy, the black space, gradually stills, while from the other side of the membrane appears, further on, the desk, the pile of books behind, against the wall, the glass with the pencils, the folder on which I am writing, in large printed letters, with red ink, hurried and irregular, PARA-NATELLON. I was and I am about to be and I am about to be about to be—in large printed letters, PARANATELLON. And now I am holding, again, in my hands, the green folder on which is written, in red ink, in large, irregular letters, hurriedly printed, PARANATELLON. And now I am putting down, again, onto the desk—without opening it?—the folder. There it is, the cold bedroom, flickering, in which each thing is, and I myself am, in the same, coming and going from somewhere even in its apparent repose, place. In the cold bedroom, flickering, there is a bed, a green desk, a folder, books, papers piled up behind, a bookshelf, flickering, coming into and going out of, as you might say, something, in the same, always, apparently, place. There they are: the bookshelf, the folder, the chair, my knees, the ashtray, the door, mute, always in the same, with the *Wheatfield with Crows* and the light softly veiled by the smoke, flickering, place. They say, you might say, nothing. Questioning: questioning, in order, one at a time, or all together, everything, questioning the desk, the folder, questioning the newspaper with the two blurry photographs that say, or seem to want to say, that is to say, nothing, questioning the bed, questioning the chair, the light, the book-shelf, questioning, again and again, the voices that spoke, the expressionless faces, the memories that my eyes, raising up, seem to go looking for—where?—and then, again, the newspaper, the two photographs, blurry, reproduced, at once, sixty-two thousand times, and then again the expressionless faces, the voices, my eyes raising up or darting from side to side, as if they were searching, outside, around, like the one who blows on a cookie in a cup of tea and brings it afterward to his mouth, for the dew, the vapor, the image, questioning the dimple, to say, so to speak, and once and for all, something, questioning the table, the plate, questioning the chair, questioning the rising and setting of the sun, the rivers, the sum-mer, questioning the leaves of books and the leaves of trees, the plains, the sand, testing, definitively, again, to see if something says, so to speak, something, questioning what is always, and since always has been, the same, indefinite, huge, with no borders to flow over or anything beyond those borders into which to over-flow, fixed, neutral, flickering, place. Blurry, the two photographs, sixty-two thousand times, ubiquitous, are, nevertheless, nothing. They show nothing. Some confused stains, black, gray, white, that seem to be a desk, a chair behind, a wall, and between the desk and the wall, in the dark stains making up the floor, the stain, slightly darker, of a body, crumpled, face down, while there is still visible, below the dark stain of hair, a little gray stain, irregular, the face: the profile, its mouth open. And then, below, the second, a white stain: the wall. And upon the white stain, four—or five?—dark little stains, somewhere between gray and black: the bullets?—and that is, or would seem to be, from all the rest, all. Questioning, still questioning: the desk, the chair, questioning the four—or five—little stains somewhere between gray and black, on the wall, questioning the body fallen and crumpled, questioning the open mouth, the head, questioning day and night, and again the dimple, the green folder, the wall, questioning the trees, the leaves on the trees, questioning the streets, the white, vacuous faces, expressionless, to see, once more, if it is possible to say, about oneself or about anything, anything. Anything about the full, waving expanse, intersected, continuous, entering and exiting, again and again, the black bath, death, resurrection, resurrected death, and again death and again resurrection, adrift, moving from and moving toward nowhere, trembling, tremblingly present, to be seen, touched, heard, breaths that are clearly here and yet which come, the table, the desk, the dimple, the body fallen and fearful, the rising and setting of the sun, the bookcase, from what world? Floating, adrift, passing by, reappearing, disintegrating, crystallizing, in an arduous, dazzling, continuous wave. Now I am lighting a cigarette, the flame rising, after a tiny explosion, toward my mouth, and the smoke floats adrift, passing, reappearing, disintegrating, crystallizing in an arduous, dazzling, continuous wave. On the black head of the match which I hold upright, between my thumb and index finger, the orange flame waves, changes, and continues to be, if you like, the same, it twists, it waves, toward the left, toward the right, straight up, it winds around itself, slowly, on the wooden tip of the match, blackening it, consuming it, the flame that now descends toward my fingers, just as, above, the black wooden tip folds, breaks into pieces and yet does not, yet, crumble, the black tip breaks, at last, in two, when the flame reaches my fingers, provoking a hurried shake of my hand, whose movement, violent, repeated, puts it out. On my light gray pants, the black ash, its hard head still intact. While the thumb and forefinger of my left hand hold up the little stub of wood with its black tip, the fingers of my right delicately retrieve the ash, the little black head, from my pants, sprinkling it out, allowing it to fall between the chair and the bookcase, onto the floor. The little pieces, the specks, are hardly visible against the yellow tile. The fingers of my right hand have been, on the pad of my thumb, on the pad and the side of my forefinger, lightly on the pad of my middle finger, blackened with ash: black stains. There remains, between the fingers of my left hand, no longer than a quarter inch, with its black tip, mute, the little piece of wood: was there, once, something else, between my fingers, besides a little piece of wood, tiny, not more than a quarter inch long, with a blackened tip? Was there, in the air, moving, alive, orange, brilliant, between my fingers, a flame? The cigarette gives off smoke, consuming itself, in the ashtray. And if there was, once, between my fingers, brilliant, in the air, orange, a flame, where was it, so to speak, in what world? Was it, was it in the midst of being, is it, is it in the midst of being, is it still, is it still in the midst of being? It was, it was in the midst of being and it was being, it is, it is in the midst of being, it is still, it is still being. The stub with the black tip falls, when my fingers cease to hold it, upon the yellow tile. Now my blackened fingers pick up the cigarette from the ash- tray, bringing it in a single, brusque motion to my mouth. For a moment nothing, so to speak, happens, nothing. From down below, from the television, there comes neither voices nor music: nothing. Nor from further away, from the streets, from the corners, from the sidewalks, from the houses, from the fixed lights that must be, in the same, in the night, in the cold, place: nothing. Nor from above, from the black air, in which shines, round, frigid, white, the moon, not there either, it would seem: nothing. There is only the smoke that rises, slowly diffusing in the bedroom, toward the light, veiling it, lightly, and the bed, the chair, the bookcase, my knees, the desk with the books, the papers piled up behind, against the yellow wall, the glass with the pencils, the pens, my hands, the picture on the wall, the green folder on which it must say, in large, irregular red letters, hurriedly printed, PARANATELLON. Emptiness, and up here, on the surface, sleepiness. Against an empty background that is not, in the strictest sense, any background at all, growing, shrinking, advancing, retreating, accumulating, drowsiness. And the convulsions that ought, by their violence, to dissipate it, are like the convulsions, of—in order to say it, I will say it this way—a dying animal, meant to startle a band of crows: a hurried flight, a fluttering return, and then, again, settling down, to devour. In reality it is unknown, now, where, so to speak, the border remains, nor where, in reality, remains reality. In, to say it somehow, the test tube of the body, the liquid, transparent or cloudy, of sleep, rises up to the eyes, it would seem, and suddenly, while not petrifying them, it coagulates them. Or an agitation, or an anthill, perhaps, that does not exactly agitate, but that expands, in order, setting out, from where? Toward the ends, from the center, toward the ends, that is, to put myself, in another, later, precise, dimension, having passed through a zone, so to speak, of turbulence. A dozing from which one could emerge—where? Or where one enters, you might say, more precisely, having emerged, and for a moment, a sort of, say, flash, from a polished, swift, precise piece of the world, that is nothing but, in memory, that which we call, or that which we believe should be, not just a piece, but the whole—the whole of—the world. Sleepiness, dozing: and the body, which should, at all times, hold fast, rests, or struggles with itself, more accurately, weak, asleep, while in front, or behind, or around, in the grayish smoke, the matter unwinds, one can, in this state, to hold fast to, that which we shall call, for the moment, nothing. Nothing from the ashtray, from the desk, from the green folder, from the two photographs, blurry, repeated, at once, sixty-two thousand times, nor from the dimple, either, nothing, except, monotonous, identical, stable, the shaking of my head. And below, successive, mobile, or immobile, perhaps, changing or identical, at all times, exceeding itself, the emptiness. Fixing my gaze on something, while my fingers bring the cigarette toward the desk and crush it, slowly, into the ashtray. Fixing my gaze. On something. While my fingers. The picture: stains, black, yellow, blue, green, reddish, gray, spinning, immobile, or stampeding, crowding each other, gathered, unstable, suspended, not of conflict, nor of ruins, but of imminence, with nothing, but nothing, neither from this side nor from the other, nothing more than a canvas of blue, yellow, green, black, gray, red (stampeding? suspended? gathering? scattering? before, during, after?) the catastrophe, if there is what we understand to be, or what should be, a catastrophe, and most importantly around what nucleus or what center: a black stain, superimposed, violently, upon a blue stain, strewn with a few broken black strokes, and below, a yellow stain divided, in the middle, by two winding green lines that, unexpectedly, almost immediately, arbitrarily, join, and below, at last, the fragments, suspended, or gathering, or stampeding. And still, the yellow stain is not entirely yellow, nor the blue stain entirely blue, nor are the green stains entirely green, nor are the red fragments entirely red, nor are the grays entirely gray, nor are the broken black strokes either entirely broken or entirely black—the green stains entirely green, nor the red fragments, the gray ones entirely, nor the black strokes, broken, no can one say, either, that there is no center, since the whole thing is, anyway, the center. The blue and black stains, above a wheat field, are supposed to be the sky, and the yellow stain, below the blue and black one that, above a wheat field, is supposed to be the sky, is supposed to be a wheat field, and the winding green lines that, arbitrarily, and suddenly, join, dividing in two the yellow stain that is supposed to be a wheat field, are supposed be a path, and the winding green, red, gray lines, that go along, without, nevertheless, joining, but rather dividing, to the left of the painting, from a common stain, the green lines that are supposed to be a path, one supposes that they, ubiquitous, are supposed to be the earth, and the broken black strokes, nervous, hurried, scattered, disorderly, stampeding, in flight, gathering, suspended, against the blue and black stain that is supposed to be the sky, against the yellow stain that is supposed to be the wheat field, are supposed to be—scattering? gathering?—crows from a common stain, the green lines that are supposed to be, one supposes, below, ubiquitous, the earth, the black strokes, hurried, nervous, stampeding, which are supposed to be, and above the blue and black stain, vague, yellowish, whitish, two circles, in an atmosphere not of catastrophe, nor of ruin, not of the day before nor the day after, but of imminence, so that before, or after, on this side, or on the other, there can be nothing, what is called nothing. Or fixing, my gaze that is, on something, on something else, and seeing, for a moment, what would be necessary, trying to force out of it, if it were even possible, for once, even if it were only a, to call it something, sign. But no, there is nothing: nothing on which to fix my gaze, nothing. Nothing I say, for the moment, nothing. And there comes, all at once, or appears, rather, all around, and right here, almost featureless, silence. Exhaustion: and silence that is—permanence? change? permanence and change? permanent change? No way—nothing, it would seem, would be disposed, on the out-side, if someone, at some time, should ask something, to respond. Nor allow, either by accident, or above all on purpose, any part, of itself or of anything else, to be glimpsed. No: silence, from this side and from the other, and from this side, stable, dense, exhaustion. On neither side, for the moment, is there a sound that could be, so to speak, interpreted, or that coming, at once, from things, appear-ing, resonating, becomes, for a fraction of a second, intelligible, a voice, or would be, to put it better, or more deliberately, if you like, in an anonymous, even impersonal, for no one in particular, and from no one in particular, to call it something, call. I stand: the chair, creaking, breaks, so to speak, into pieces, for a moment, the silence, which at once, immediately, snaps shut again. I am stand-ing, immobile, between the chair and the desk, beneath the light that the smoke, lightly, veils, and from below, from outside, no voice comes, no music, either, no sound, from the television. From outside, from below, now that I am standing, immobile, between the desk and the chair, from the place where they have been, or are still, and may, very well, still be being, even when they are, now, in the darkness of the bedroom, lying, no sound comes, no voice. Now that I am opening the door there comes, along with the cold unmoving air of June, from the far off clock, dark, imperceptible, a chime. Immobile again, in that door between the lit bedroom, full of smoke, hot, with the chair, the desk, the bed, the bookshelf, and the frigid terrace, bright, transparent, over which keeps watch, so to speak, from up above, icy, smooth, the moon. The echo of the chime resounds, for some moments, fleetingly, in me. It has said, even so, to me, and even having wanted, probably, to say something, nothing in particular: it could have been the chime for one o'clock, or for one thirty, or for quarter to two, or for quarter to one, or for twelve thirty, or for twelve fifteen, or also, probably—and why not?—the last stroke of midnight; or the last of eleven o'clock, or eleven fifteen, or even, probably, eleven thirty, or, much more likely, even, and probably, a quarter to twelve. I am standing at the doorway, between the bedroom and the terrace. And I am still being, but not, at the same time, seated in the chair. Am I still being, and not at the same time, seated in the chair? Am I still being seated in the chair and am I still being standing immobile on one side of the chair with the echo of the creak that has broken, for a moment, the silence, and am I still being crossing the space between the chair and the door, and am I still being hearing, as I open the door, dull, far off, the chime, while I am existing, immobile, standing, looking in the direction of the cold darkness, in the doorway between the bedroom and the terrace? Am I? Am I still? And if I am, if I am still, where am I and am I still, in what world? In one from which there comes, for now, no call. No voice, in effect, to obey, nor, to direct, so to speak, when I move, my footsteps: no,

I am standing, immobile, not going anywhere, in the doorway, looking toward the terrace at what is watched over by, from above, frigid, the moon, my back to the illuminated bedroom onto which the smoke settles, delicately, a mist, and I have been crossing, slowly, the space between the chair and the door, I have been opening the door, I have been standing immobile for a moment next to the chair, I have been standing up from the chair, having been seated, in silence, and still failing to hear, from anywhere, what I would say is, what we may say is, what we could call, austerely, a direction, immediately, imperceptibly, almost inaudible, coming from outside, a call. Nor does a call move me now, to cross, so to speak, the doorway, taking a step, just one step, toward the terrace, toward the cold, to cross, as if for the first time, or, plain and simple, for the first time, the threshold: and there is, there is an inaudible roar, when I pass, without the bookshelf, without the chair, without the desk, without the *Wheatfield with Crows*, the light lightly veiled by the smoke, into the other place. It is other and, even so, it is, and no bigger, the same—moving? still?—place. Nor does a call, now, fix me in this place, immobile, make me turn now, and make me, now, cross again, in the opposite direction—and why direction? why opposite?—the, to call it something, threshold. And if there were, that is, what we could call, so to speak, a meaning, that is, a break, arbitrary, laughable, in the huge stain that moves—how? where? and most of all: why?—if there were, between two points, one that we could call the beginning, the other the end, or, respectively, the cause and the effect, one could say that, without receiving a call, without a purpose, I pass, from the beginning to the end, from the illuminated bedroom to the frigid terrace, I return, you might say, through the doorway, and, with no call having intervened, no call, from end to beginning, from effect, so to speak, to cause, from the dark, cold terrace to the bedroom whose light, tenuously, is veiled by smoke, then no one, but no one, could really say how, or where, or when, or, most of all, why. Now I am standing immobile, my back to the terrace, beneath the light enveloped in smoke, facing the yellow wall, at one point in the room, between the chair and the door. At one point. In the room. Between the chair. And the door. At one point in the room, between the chair and the door. At one point? At one point in the room? Between the chair? Between the chair and the door? At one point in the room between the chair and the door? I am existing, standing, facing the terrace now, the open door, at a point in the room, that is, in turn, at some point, immobile, that is in turn at some point, between the chair and the door. Now I am crossing, slowly, so to speak, the doorway: and there resounds, in the air, for the first time, inaudible, the roar: but no, no, not the first: it re-sounds, nothing more, inaudible, the roar, as I cross, so to speak, slowly, the doorway. The cold air touches, or brushes, or settles onto my cheeks. I go forth, slowly, toward the center of the terrace, below the moon: frigid, round, yellow, keeping watch, all around, over the stars. And all in a circle, and all around, the city: another, at some point, with its dark blocks, its files of streetlamps, its tree-lined patios, its subtle sounds, permanent, or changing, perhaps, chaotic, silent, place. And the lights, in the vast, tranquil darkness, indicate, each one, in its spot, a fixed, limited, brilliant, place. There is, certainly, somewhere, behind me, another point, illuminated, with the desk, the chair, the bookcase, the green folder on which I have written, in large red, irregular, hurriedly printed letters, PARA-NATELLON. Is there, somewhere, illuminated, full of smoke, with the light, the bed, the picture, and the chair, that place? From the moon, with its frigid light, there descends, so to speak, no sound. And I think, moreover, of nothing. For the moment, now, no sound, nothing. No bird, singing, in the darkness, up above, to somewhere else, standing out, for a moment, black, sharp, against the sky, and no sign, either, that something, at this moment, might be about, you might say, in the sky, or here, around, to move, or to flutter: nothing. Nor any shadow disengaging itself, so to speak, from the shade, nor changing smoothly, its place: not that either: nothing. Except, naturally, exhaustion, and above, round, frigid, keeping watch, all around, and for the moment, over the stars, the moon. The cold coils around me. The cold that should have, that should, rather, or perhaps, I don't know anymore, that would, if you will, or that, probably, having crossed from the heat of the room, the enclosed space, through the doorway, and hitting, suddenly, my cheeks, that should have, it seems, diminished, you might say, has, on the contrary, in effect, increased, on my face, or, perhaps, behind it, paradoxically, my sleepiness. That is the way it should have been, as usual, apparently diminishing as I stepped outside, and yet, on the contrary, apparently, or more precisely you might say that, on my face, or more precisely behind, it had been, so to speak, precisely, increased. Wandering, floating, or immobile, perhaps, the darkness brings, frozen, in a continual flow, the moon, the stars, lights, blocks, trees, around, and brings them back, slowly, again, giving the illusion, paradoxically, of motionlessness, floating around, stars, lights, trees. Unexpectedly, on the contrary, and from somewhere else, rather than having, as might be expected, effectively, diminished, it seems to have, the sleepiness, behind, or inside, better now, clearly, having gone, from the illuminated bedroom, slowly, through the doorway, in the darkness, sharply, to have increased. Crossing, coming, or settling onto, already, in the darkness, opening up, so to speak, the cold, in solidarity with my sleepiness, or even better, one with it, envelopes me, now, increasing it and not, as it should have, diminishing it. Everything is one. It seems possible now to make out nothing: there would seem to have been, effectively, so to speak, no separation, nor, would there seem to be, as it seems that there should be, an inside, an in front, an outside, an in back, an, imaginary, all around: no, nothing. Out in the cold darkness are, so to speak, the terrace, and also the moon, and swept together, chaotically, strewn about, the black patios, and the trees, the houses, the lights, the stars as well, cold, green, immobile, everything inside, probably, of something and traveling—wandering, you might say, more precisely, and, without, to say it somehow, direction, and without, for the moment, cohesion, the mass curve that seems to continually consume itself, and continues, nevertheless, to be the same, and that being, nevertheless, fixed, in place, at all times, in its own place—toward what?— passes, it would seem, hurriedly in a certain sense, and departs. Everything, for the moment, it seems, would be, you might say, one: without, so to speak, any particularity, with no inside, or outside, and no, so to speak, delightful, happy, diversity—the flow, without intermissions, without rhythm, without origin, which now, so to speak, drifts, and which will be, it would seem, always, the same, with its moons, its stars, its abandoned blocks, its cold terraces, the desk, the chair, the bookshelf, the point between the chair and the door, reincarnating itself, consuming itself—where? when? and most of all, why?—to call it something, place. It is, for the moment, being, as you might say, continuous, entire, in its place: exhaustion, useless, fragmented, leaving no impression, a magma, to express it somehow, and nothing, but nothing, to take from it. I am seemingly standing, then, immobile, on the cold terrace, it would seem, yes, momentarily, yet I am able to take, from all of this, nothing. It is a state that, you might say, should not be, or should not have been, anyway, in the condition, or perhaps the node, or the root, should not have been, or should not, rather, and yet, it seems, apparently, to confuse, or fuse, erasing the limits, if the expression could, at this moment, say, precisely, something, it should not have, I have said, or should not, would not have been, really, apparently, confused or fused. One could say, so to speak, somehow, flowing, and being, once again, always, in the same place, there is nothing left to flow, no other—no other, that is, somewhere else, where it is not flowing, fixed, as I have said, place. And now I am turning around, I am leaving behind the moon, the stars, and chaotic, silent, the city. I am, at this moment, turning, leaving, so to speak, behind me, guarded, the stars, the moon, and chaotic, in chiaroscuro, the city. And I continue, so to speak, to move forward, to the left, on the inside now—in what world?—to the right, passing, and not just in space—to what place?—to the left, once again an abyss, the right again and again everything, everything remains, so to speak, forever, behind me: moving forward, immobile, blurry, in the darkness, in the cold, having erased, imperceptibly, the limits: inside, outside, below, above, around, before, now, after. The left, the right, the left, the right, the left, the right: floating, wandering, never hearing what we call, to call it something, a call, that imposes, arbitrarily, what you might call, so to speak, a direction, in some part, sleepiness, nodding, with nothing startling to bring forth an awakening, and what stands out, despite all of this, is the exhaustion, as if it were, or as if it were possible to be certain that there is, or that there could be, in another moment, another state. It is, it would seem, or is being, really, although it would be, really, difficult, if you like, to fix it in a given moment, right then, right there, it would seem, without it having to declare, as usual, in that continuous, curved, perhaps, flow, in which slowly, ravaged, blindly, it drifts, where it should have been, or should be, really, would have, yes, or no, should have been, really, should have, yes, or should? Yes, or no, actually, I've said should have, crossing, although if I had remained I would have, anyway, in a certain sense, stayed in it, the doorway, with the fragile, inaudible roar, that should, or should have, yes, should have, instead of, unexpectedly, I said, and perhaps, also, somehow, to call it something, imperceptibly, increased, that should have, I have said, crossing, having stood in the darkness, before the frigid, round, white moon, with the rooftops in confusion all around, the patios, floating, wandering—toward what?—giving the possibility, improbably, somewhere else, of a change of state, lightly, or gradually, even, against my cheeks, or behind, really, inside, has in fact diminished. Crossing the threshold now, and entering, so to speak, the illuminated bedroom. I am existing standing in the illuminated room, now, before the bed: and now I am taking off, carelessly, the blue wool jacket and hanging it on the back of the chair, taking off, slowly, my tie, unbuttoning the collar of my shirt. The tie, with wide diagonal stripes, gray and blue, I hang now on the back of the chair, over the blue jacket. Now I am taking off my white pullover, I am still taking off the white pullover, I am yanking the white pullover up to get it over my head, yanking it by the collar, and for a moment, now, for a moment, I see the illuminated room through the thick knit of the wool which transforms the whole space into a grid, pockmarked, really, with luminous points and black ones. And now I am putting down, after having arranged it a bit, pulling out the sleeves and folding it, the white pullover on top of the jacket and the tie, on the back of the chair. Now I am standing in shirtsleeves, fixed between the bed and the chair, in the illuminated room. There is, it seems, something that would like, so to speak, to come. It seems. Like a head of something that stretches up from below, from the bottom, really, just now: but no, nothing. Immobile, in the illuminated bedroom that is hard, inalterable, cold, guarded by the smoke, with the bed, the chair, the bookshelf—the same? always?—place. And now, still standing, I am using my heels to take off my shoes. My feet, so to speak, in blue socks, touch, now, the icy tile. My hands unfasten my belt, unbutton, unhurriedly, my fly: I am taking off, balancing first on my right leg, now on my left, lifting them to fold them over carefully, trying to match up the legs, and depositing them on top of the white pullover, on the back of the chair, still warm, my pants. I have said that

I was taking off, carelessly, the blue wool jacket, and, I have said, hanging it on the back of the chair. And I have said: that I took off, slowly, my tie, that I undid the collar of my shirt, the tie with the wide diagonal stripes, gray and blue, the white shirt, hanging it on the back of the chair, on top of the blue jacket. That I yanked up, by the collar, my white pullover, to get it over my head, I have said, and that I saw for a moment, through the wool mesh that enveloped me, so to speak, I have said, the whole room transformed into a pockmarked image of luminous points and black ones. That I stood for a moment, fixed, so to speak, in the room. And I said, that there after having seemed, for a moment, that there was something that, as you might say, was trying to, or, deceptively, appearing to appear, I took off, using my heels, my shoes. I stepped onto the frozen tile in my blue socks, while my hands unfastened, unhurriedly, my belt, my fly, and I said that balancing first on my right leg, then on my left, lifting them to fold them over carefully, trying to match up the legs, and depositing them on top of the white pullover, on the back of the chair, still warm, gray flannel, my pants. And now I am unbuttoning the white shirt, shivering. My underwear, my blue socks, are now, on the yellow tile, three dark mounds. I am, for a second, immobile, completely naked, shivering: in the illuminated room, cold, between the ceiling and the yellow tile, between the yellow walls, naked, for a second, or a fraction of a second, really, sleepy, shivering. A second or a fraction of a second, adrift, inside of something sleepy, shivering. My entire skin, surrounded, entirely, by the air, squeezed by it, so to speak, and more than a moment, it is a state: or the beginning, perhaps, or the pretext, really, for a beginning, because earlier, others could: they would wet, slowly, thoroughly, bringing it afterward to their mouths, in the cup of tea, the cookie, they would let the sugared dough dissolve on the tip of their tongues, and from the contact would come, fiercely, wafting up—from what world?—memory. And now I am taking, from under the pillow, folded up, my orange frieze pajamas. And now, dressed in my pajamas, I am getting in between the frozen sheets, shivering. I am inside. And my hand, coming out from between the frozen sheets, slides along, brushing the rough surface of the yellow wall until it finds, smooth, the light switch. Now I am in the most perfect darkness. Nothing is visible, nothing, neither inside, nor outside, what is called nothing: and yet something happens, deliberately, so to speak, in the blackness, despite the apparent, not and just superficial, immobility. For a moment, as you might say, nothing happens, although I know—since when?—that something, inside, or inside of whatever, so to speak, makes the blackness flicker, is happening: in the most arduous darkness. And to see, now, it seems, yes, to see, out of this nothingness, if it is possible, like others, like before, to extract, like a dream, so to speak, a memory of something: because earlier, others could: they would wet, slowly, in the afternoon, in the kitchen, in the winter, the cookie in the cup of tea, they would bring it to their mouths and deposit it on the tip of their tongues, and from there, suddenly, or gradually, from the tongue, or from the sugared dough, from somewhere, like a vapor from the swamp, would rise, victorious, precise, memory, the memory that, not even knowing what memory is, nor if there is something, outside, to remember, could be the foundation, in the blackness, of something. To see something now: something that, while not the beginning, nevertheless, would serve to begin, or as an example of that which, having begun, would continue. To see, so to speak, to see something, I have said. To see, though your eyes might have, before them, nothing. I am, then, in the darkness, and looking, paying attention, I see rise, slowly, from the swamp, like a memory, the vapor: in a corner of the city, or of the mind, or to a corner, really, of the city, always, or of the mind, as I have said, so to speak, a moment ago, if moment can still, so to speak, mean, what comes coming—from where?—into a corner of the city, then, into the noonday sun, slowly, I float. I must be me, because I am myself, it seems, the one remembering. And the whole corner, with its sun, its crosswalks, its shop windows, the short shadows projecting onto the gray sidewalk, the cars, their chrome, fast, flashing, the houses, the bus full of students turning, slowly, from Mendoza onto San Martín, rise now from the swamp, shining, phosphorescent, wandering for a moment, and then fading. Nothing, now, and everything black again: and again, now, from below, from the bottom, if it is even conceivable that there is, so to speak, a bottom, the four corners, in the noonday sun, and the bodies that move, or are immobile, in the sun, the shop windows, the cars, the bus full of students that looks like it is from another city, inside of which one of the students, crouching, aims his camera at the sunny sidewalk toward which I am floating, slowly, toward the corner, shining, wandering, and nothing now: everything is black again. In the arduous or neutral, really, darkness, one realizes that, even so, something passes, and it seems it would be easier, if you like, to stop it than to find, in the confusion of the hours between murky visions, in the reluctance, a reason, ironclad, constant, and luminous, to want it: flowing, if you like, constantly, because, even eroding us, it can, so to speak, take nothing from us, since it would seem that there is nothing, or that we were given nothing, but nothing, to be taken. And it rises, now, tenacious, like a sun, in the sun again, the memory: the gray pavement onto which the short, passing shadows are neatly stamped, the four corners where people gather together, be they unemployed men warmed by pullovers of every color, who have been there since at least eleven watching the women who shuttle around San Martín dart again and again in and out of shops, or the store employees who have just gotten off work and who either stand idling in the sun or set out in every direction, toward Salta, in the south, toward Primera Junta, in the north, toward 25 de Mayo, in the east, toward

San Jerónimo, in the west, to wait, almost certainly, for the bus, to go, almost certainly, home for lunch, the shop windows, perfectly arranged, resplendent, the shoe stores, the corner stores, the fabric shops, the candy and cigarette kiosks, the Gran Doria Bar, whose daytime darkness contrasts with the sparkling brilliance of the exterior, its clients, who drink coffee or vermouth, have seated themselves strategically so as to be able to see, through the large windows, what is happening on the street, inside the bus turning, as I am flowing onto the corner, south, toward Salta, the inside of the bus where one of the students, crouching in his seat by the window, points his camera in the direction where I, on the gray sidewalk, am heading along Mendoza, from west to east, coming upon San Martín, sheathed, deliberately, in my black overcoat, while a man, turning from San Martín onto Mendoza, a man in a gray hat and an overcoat of the same color, from whose collar peeps a yellow scarf, steps aside for me, politely, among the clamor of voices and car motors and laughter, and from the doors that close and open, and from the footsteps that scrape against the sidewalk, and the key rings men jingle in their gloved hands, if hands, if key rings, if scarf, if me, if San Martín, if west, if shop windows, if brilliance, if store, if shadows, if corner—can, now, and again, mean, as you might say, and if you would permit the expression, something. There are also, so to speak, four corners in my mind, in my memory. And from the lower right-hand corner I am coming, slowly, to San Martín, and in the other corner, on the diagonal, in the upper left-hand corner, the patrons of the Gran Doria, sitting in the daytime darkness of the café that contrasts sharply with the brilliance of the exterior, watch, smoking thoughtfully, the street; staggering by and piling up between the other two corners are pedestrians, cars, the bus full of students, the two intersecting streets, the shop windows, and above everything, the sparkling blue sky—if sparkling, if everything, if students, if café, if daytime, have, even in my memory, even in my mind, some, so to speak, meaning. And I am existing always, now, in the blackness, in the same, floating, wandering, inside of something, or in something that passes along with the mobile memory that rises, disappears and comes back, stubbornly, victorious, to rise, from the swamp, uncertain, changing and resting, shrunken, frozen, unapproachable, from within or from without, place. In the corners of my memory, mobile, confused, there are, toward the center, clearer, the stains of the morning that move, the black, green, yellow, blue, white, gray stains, stains of the luminous morning that float, changing, not simply, like living organisms, their form, but also, and always, their place: the blue sky, full of sparkling splinters, smooth, from above the gray or white houses, the cars advancing slowly along Mendoza, from west to east, red, white, green, blue, black, yellow, their motors revving in first, the shouts and the laughter, the voices, the footsteps scraping against the sidewalk, the metal grating that screech sharply closed, the key rings jingling in gloved hands, the shop windows, perfectly arranged, the horns, the daytime darkness of the Gran Doria, through whose large windows its patrons, slowly drinking vermouth or coffee, abstractly consider, smoking unhurriedly, the street, the women who pass by, their shopping done, saddled with packages under their arms, beneath the gaze of men wrapped in pullovers that are blue, green, white, maroon, lilac, red, who smoke under the sun, leaning against windows or standing, upright, on the curb, the sky-blue bus full of students that must have come, surely, to visit the city, inside of which one of the students, crouched in his seat, barely keeping his balance as the bus tilts, turning from Mendoza to San Martín, to the south, points his camera, which obscures the greater part of his face, toward the corner, the point on the gray sidewalk where I am flowing from San Martín, just about to obligate the man in the yellow scarf to step aside, yielding to me, at noon, in the sun, in the street, in the luminous winter—and the borders, crumbling, or graying, really, of the memory, move, stretch, or shrink, the memory that has been rising up, so to speak, from the black, and that flickers, patently, at the heart of the abyss, as if it were saying, or as if it were, really, trying to say, that there *is* something, something, from which to derive, so to speak, evidence to the contrary, the negation of the negation that there has been, at some point, noon, winter, the daytime darkness of the Gran Doria from which silent men observe, as they smoke, the street through picture windows, a bus from another city inside of which a student points his camera at the sidewalk, four corners bathed in a brilliant roar, and above all, floating from Mendoza to San Martín, the thing that would bring, like a black vessel, with its cars, its windows, its sounds, its yellow scarf, its frozen light, to this point, this memory. And as if it were possible to know, if it really is memory, of what, exactly, it is a memory: that is, what could there be in common, so to speak, between a yellow scarf, and the memory that rises—from what world?—yellow, in the form of a scarf that extends, now, from that corner into the center. It seems that there would be, or should be, really, nothing in common between those two yellow stains, the one I remember, the one I remember remembering, or the one that I believe, really, seeing it appear, that I remember, and the one that has been outside, in another place, in another time, no bridge, no, so to speak, relation. And concerning the men that, I think I have said, appear to me, in the daytime darkness of the Gran Doria, smoking, drinking coffee, I know, really, so to speak, nothing: I couldn't say, probably, at this distance, if they are drinking, really, coffee, or if they are smoking, or if they are, really, men, unless they cling to, so to speak, in this emptiness, memories that are, ultimately, memories of nothing, of nothing in particular, and I couldn't even say of them that they are, really, in the precise meaning of the word, if a word should have, by obligation, a precise meaning, memories. The cup, moreover, of coffee that is supposedly rising, at this very moment, to my lips, would be, in reality, in memory, not a cup, and the coffee, not coffee, no quantity of black liquid, steaming, covered in golden foam, that has not filled anything, anywhere, and has never passed to nowhere, having been swallowed by no one, bitter, lukewarm, down no throat: no, there is, in the memory of that coffee, no coffee, and the yellow scarf, which should be the source of the yellow stain that rises now, alone, from the swamp, floats, disintegrating—where is it, in what world, or in what worlds?

Translator's Acknowledgments

My most profound thanks to all the people who have supported this translation along the way: To Michelle Clayton, who first introduced me to this strange and wonderful book. To Anne Jump, Johanna McKeon, and David Rieff at the Susan Sontag Foundation for seeing the potential in it. Most especially, to Michael Henry Heim, for inspiring me to follow this path. You are deeply missed.

I also owe a debt of gratitude to the family and friends who have supported me through various drafts of this translation. I especially thank my twin sister Sonja Sharp, the Cat to my Pigeon; my dear friend Rebecca Lippman, who has indulged me in so many literary arguments; and my husband Hayden Kantor, my most careful and constant reader.

Juan José Saer was the leading Argentinian writer of the post-Borges generation. The author of numerous novels and short-story collections (including *Scars* and *La Grande*), Saer was awarded Spain's prestigious Nadal Prize in 1987 for *The Event*.

Roanne L. Kantor is a doctoral student in Comparative Literature at the University of Texas at Austin. Her translation of *The One Before* won the 2009 Susan Sontag Prize for Translation. Her translations from Spanish have appeared in *Little Star* magazine, *Two Lines,* and *Palabras Errantes: Latin American Literature in Translation.*

Open Letter—the University of Rochester's nonprofit, literary translation press—is one of only a handful of publishing houses dedicated to increasing access to world literature for English readers. Publishing ten titles in translation each year, Open Letter searches for works that are extraordinary and influential, works that we hope will become the classics of tomorrow.

Making world literature available in English is crucial to opening our cultural borders, and its availability plays a vital role in maintaining a healthy and vibrant book culture. Open Letter strives to cultivate an audience for these works by helping readers discover imaginative, stunning works of fiction and poetry, and by creating a constellation of international writing that is engaging, stimulating, and enduring.

Current and forthcoming titles from Open Letter include works from Bulgaria, China, France, Greece, Iceland, Israel, Latvia, Poland, South Africa, and many other countries.

www.openletterbooks.org